HAPPENSTANCE

HAPPENSTANCE

Hal Barwood

gambling on democracy

Happenstance

Acknowledgments . . .

Many thanks to the readers who bravely tackled early versions of this tale; especially Barbara Barwood, Jonathan Barwood, Tobias Barwood, Betsy Blanchard, Curt Blanchard, Louis Castle, Robert Dalva, Beverly Graves, and Matthew Robbins.

Thanks always to Google, Wikipedia, and the rest of the World Wide Web for reminding the author that anything can happen.

About the Author . . .

Hal Barwood is a veteran writer with multiple credits in multiple media. Find out more here . . .

www.finitearts.com

for
Betsy & Curt
friends old and dear

Table of Contents

July   1
Chapters 1 2 3 4 5 6 7 8

August   41
Chapters 9 10 11 12 13 14 15 16 17

September   75
Chapters 18 19 20 21 22 23 24 25 26 27 28

October   121
Chapters 29 30 31 32 33 34 35 36 37 38 39 40

November   183
Chapters 41 42 43 44 45 46 47 48 49 50

JULY

1

"HEY TEAM, you see that? Down there, third row."

In the shadowy surveillance offices of the *Silverlode Casino and Sports Book* on North Virginia Street in Reno, Nevada, a junior security agent was jabbing his finger at a glowing TV screen.

"Get over here and check out the baseball cap — this guy, he's robbing us blind."

The rest of the security force rose from their chairs and gathered around their colleague's closed-circuit TV monitor to observe the behavior of a customer working the slot machines on the floor below. The flurry of activity caused the shift manager, Jennifer Penrose, a handsome blonde woman in chic business attire, to follow her crew.

"What's the damage?" she wondered.

"Around three thousand bucks, all in less than an hour."

"Lucky guy, huh?"

"Lucky? Shit. He stands around, looking, looking, looking — then he sits down, wins a while, pulls his ticket, moves along. Rinse and repeat."

"You've seen this before? Do we know him?"

"Oh yeah, we do." The junior security agent picked up a clipboard and studied his notes "I got a face match. Biometrics shows him as Michael Solano. He's here almost every day. Mostly sports book, but now and then . . ."

". . . now and then he samples our slots."

"Yeah. And he always wins."

Dick Worden, a battle-scarred senior manager, wandered out of his office, attracted by the buzz.

"He's cheating," proclaimed Worden, fingering a bolo tie. He was dressed like a ranch hand in a denim jacket and leather boots. "What's the slot?"

"Today? *Wood Maiden, Dragon Island, Jade Kingdom,* then a different

Dragon Island, and now, *Star Wars Ultimatum.* Dollars and up."

"Fucking cheating. Some kind of spoon."

"How? How could he cheat?" Penrose was offended by the suggestion. "Those machines are tight, they're clean."

The junior security agent scanned through his notes. "Listen to
this — Solano's a VIP, one of our book's high rollers. He places a lot
of bets, does well for himself, knows his way around professional
sports. But a few years ago the prick was working for *HighScore.* One
of their coders."

Worden took the clipboard and examined the notes. He frowned.
"Is *Star Wars Ultimatum* a HighScore machine?"

Penrose shook her head. "No, Dick, TGC. It's bulletproof."

"Well, fuck me," said Worden.

Penrose's brow wrinkled. "You know, I might have met our man,
serving drinks in the book."

"Okay, Jen — get dressed and get down there. Cash him out, and
I'll read him the riot act."

"In costume? Come on, I don't work the floor these days," protested Penrose.

"Today you do. No beef. I don't want our *paying* customers stam-
peded. I swear this guy is cheating. Go! Before we're down another
couple thou."

▼

On the casino floor, bathed in the garish light of video slot machines, oblivious to the stench of stale cigarette smoke and the grumpy
hum of other players losing their money, Michael Solano was on a
roll. *Star Wars Ultimatum* was paying him fifty dollars or better just
about every other spin. A small crowd gathered to admire his performance.

Into this happy group strode Penrose, clad in little more than pasties
and a thong. She was balancing a tray of drinks with one hand. She
bent over Solano and held out a margarita.

"Compliments of the house, Mr. Solano."

The possibility of liquor spilling over his shirt front caused Solano to sit back and take notice, interrupting his rhythm.

"What? Damn, I'm in the middle of something here."

"We have a winner, don't we folks?" gurgled Penrose cheerfully. She handed drinks to the nearest of Solano's fans.

Solano sipped his margarita, pressed a button for another spin. He looked up at the woman leaning over him.

"Jenny Penny! Well, hello there, haven't seen you on patrol for a while. And by the way, it's Mickey to my friends."

Penrose's attitude sharpened abruptly. "I'm not your friend," she hissed. "You should cash out. Your lucky streak is over."

Solano gestured toward the video screen. "I don't see it. Hey, old Darth there, he just gave up fifty galactic credits."

"Cash. Out. Now."

Solano's eyes narrowed. "Listen, babe, I am one of your best customers. Go cool off some other dude and leave me alone."

The onlookers, sensing trouble, edged away. Penrose reached past Solano and pushed the *Cash Out* button. Solano's ticket rolled into view. She snapped it up. "Follow me, scout. Dick Worden wants to talk to you."

Solano reluctantly pushed his ticket through the slot in the cashier's window, tapping the counter while waiting for his money. Just as the cash appeared, so did a very angry Dick Worden. In his western outfit, the man looked more like a cowboy than a casino employee. He planted knuckles on Solano's chest and pushed. Solano grinned stupidly and retreated, being careful to stuff thirty-five hundred dollars into his jeans as he did so.

"Okay, punk, you're out of here," said Worden.

Solano shrugged. "Why is that? I like it here. Do a lot of business here."

"I don't give a shit. You're cheating, robbing my casino."

Solano stared defiantly at the casino manager, undeterred by his pock-marked face and menacing eyes. "You believe that crap? Call the cops, why don't you?"

"We never involve the police in matters like this. We handle things *internally*, understand?"

"Try it. Then I'll be the one calling the cops." Solano looked around the room, angry in his turn, attempting to contain his temper. "And, mister whoever-the-hell-you-are, know this — I'm a fairly big player in your book over there." He jerked his thumb. "You guys are doing well by me, ask your supervisor."

"Listen, you little turd, show up on our property again, and you'll fall off a loading dock in a drunken stupor, *capiche?*"

Solano knotted his hands into fists. But before he could reply to defend his reputation, a well-groomed older man in a soft gray suit floated smoothly across the floor. He placed an arresting hand on Worden's arm.

"I'll take it from here, Dick."

Worden looked at the new arrival, his boss evidently, nodded respectfully, and walked away.

"Now then . . . Mr. Solano, Michael, yes?"

Solano couldn't quite figure out the hand-off and the unexpectedly affable tone of inquiry from this fatherly figure. "It's Mickey," he said.

"Mickey, unh-huh. I'm Ed Barber, I run this place. I don't think we've met."

Solano shook his head. "Not that I remember." He stifled the impulse to add a respectful *sir* to his reply.

Barber turned, gestured for Solano to follow, and led the way to a cocktail lounge tucked into an alcove along the casino wall.

"Why don't we sit down and talk this over." The lounge was empty in the middle of the day. Barber selected a small table in the corner. "Sit," he said.

Solano eased into the chair opposite Barber, who made a big armwave to summon a waitress.

"What'll it be, gentlemen?" asked the waitress, who turned out to be Jenny Penny.

"Scotch for me, Jen. Mickey?"

Solano scowled at the woman. "You get around, lady. Just water."

Penrose sashayed away and came back with the ordered drinks. She smiled sweetly as she opened a bottle of Pellegrino and poured it into a little glass. "Lime?"

Solano pointed. Penrose squeezed, then casually flicked her wet fingers at him before striding away.

"Love your girl, there, Mr. Barber."

"Isn't she cute," said the casino manager, ignoring the sarcasm. "Now then, Mickey. I understand you have been giving our slot machines a beating this afternoon. On other afternoons as well."

Solano sipped his water. "True."

In Barber's eyes, Solano was a green kid, thin, not very tall, a cocky adolescent in a T-shirt.

"My people wonder how you get away with it. I wonder too."

"I'm a very lucky guy," allowed Solano with wary confidence. He was actually thirty-three years old, comfortably at home in casinos, and he knew a thing or two about gambling. Not really a kid at all.

"Forgive my assistant's rude manners. He's excitable, but very smart. He thinks you've got some kind of electronic spoon going."

"He's wrong. I'm just another player."

"Really. Most of my customers gradually lose money over time. You, on the other hand, consistently win. I talked to Eric over in our book. You're a VIP. I understand you're a millionaire."

Solano nodded. "Sports betting is a skill. You know that."

"Right, that's why we just take a fee. We don't care who wins or loses. But our slots — we did some investigating. You used to work for HighScore. Is that where you figured out how to cheat?"

Solano smiled. "I never play HighScore machines."

"Why is that?"

"I am — was, anyway — a computer programmer. I wrote most of the random number generators HighScore uses. They are the best."

"What I'd like to do," said Barber, toying with his glass, "is discuss your future with this company. Come to an equitable arrangement."

"Arrangement" — Solano smiled again — "I get the sense you're not actually going to throw me out."

"Not at all, not at all. You get the pleasure and profit of our facilities . . . and in return, you do us a favor."

Solano sat back, smile erased. "What kind of favor?"

"We'd like you to make a big bet, or a series of lesser bets in our book —"

"What I do anyway."

"— and lose."

Solano shook his head emphatically. "Are you nuts?"

"Pick whatever teams you like. We'll record the bets however the loss shows up."

Solano's face became ashen. "No way. I'm on the up and up."

"Hold on, son, your wealth is safe. Your bank — Nevada National? Your company — *Sporting Insights LLC?*"

"That's me."

"Take a look. You'll find a million dollars on deposit that wasn't there yesterday."

"You're kidding."

"Merry Christmas."

"What the fuck? Where did the money come from? Macau? The Cayman Islands?"

Barber lifted an eyebrow. "When you win a bet, you win big. Picked the Wimbledon bracket, how about that?"

"I never bet on tennis players. Too many drugs. Or the drug-powered Tour de France, just so you know."

"Our bookkeeper doesn't make mistakes. I looked at the receipts, and it's down there in black and white. Big win. Congratulations."

Barber leaned forward, elbows on the table, hands clasped below his chin. He extended a finger toward Solano and held his gaze with hooded eyes, revealing a hard core under the soft exterior.

"Your job is to lose that money back to us."

Solano looked around the casino. Across the room video slots were ringing up wins and losses. Cards were falling in the blackjack games. Dice were bouncing on the craps tables. Behind a glass enclosure, poker players were outwitting each other. Business as usual, but suddenly Solano felt as if reality were being yanked out from under him, like a rug.

"I can't believe what I'm hearing," he said. "Jesus. You want me to clean up your steaming pile of offshore bullshit."

"Don't be crude, Mickey. It's business. With your history as a high roller, your record of success, you are uniquely well-positioned to offer an important service."

Solano stood up, paced around the little lounge, lifted his baseball cap, ran a hand through his hair. Then he stopped and faced the casino man.

"Suppose I do this . . ."

Barber raised his hands, turned them palms up. "There's really no choice, Mickey."

"Okay, then, what's in it for me?"

Barber gestured him closer. "Don't be standoffish. Some of the bets are bound to go your way. You'll do well. We take care of our own, you'll see."

"Suppose I say *no.* 'Cause that's me. I'm no criminal."

"Sit, sit. Calm down. We're offering a generous deal. You're rich? We'll make you a lot richer."

Solano did not sit. "Sorry, Mr. Barber. I don't like your offer."

Barber sighed. "It's a good one, you'd be foolish to pass it up. But be aware, if you decline, trouble will follow."

"Oh yeah? How's that? You'll break my legs?"

"Dick, the ape man you just met, would happily drown you in the Truckee River. But I will restrain him," said Barber. He spun a finger in the air to outline a scheme. "Instead, we'll 1099 you for, say, a million over your actual winnings this year."

Solano was incredulous. "Fake my income? You can't do that."

"We can do anything."

"Wait'll I tell the Gaming Control Board."

"Go ahead. And be sure to tell your story to the IRS when they audit your taxes. Then spend a few years re-thinking your business strategy at Club Fed out in Lompoc, how's that sound?"

Solano mulled the situation. Gambling was edgy in federal law. Players with big winnings could easily become the targets of zealous prosecutors, and he had no desire to defend his life in court, let alone spend time in jail. He felt his moral compass spinning like a roulette wheel.

"This will take all week, maybe a month."

Barber shrugged agreeably. "What's that old rule? Be quick, but never in a hurry."

2

SOLANO STUMBLED out of the Silverlode onto Virginia Street in a daze. He was used to taking chances, but he hated taking orders, and he hated to lose. Now he was being ordered — ordered! — to do just that. Lose. *Be a loser.* He blinked in the light of the blazing summer sun, trying to calm down, get his bearings.

Half a block away, one of the local TV stations had set up an outpost. A technician was idly adjusting a digital video camera up on sticks under a wide sun shield. Standing beside him was a striking young woman with a KNVR-TV logo on her shirt and a wireless microphone in her hand. She spotted Solano as he exited the casino, noticed he was a good-looking guy, noticed he was carrying a long skateboard under his arm. She nudged her colleague.

"Hey, Al."

Solano was staring off into space trying, without success, to imagine a way out of his predicament. He was an adult, and he had acquired some of an adult's guarded feel for life's ups and downs, but he had yet to shed all the habits of youth. When no reasonable idea presented itself, he took a deep breath, turned his baseball cap around backwards, dropped his longboard onto the concrete, and launched himself down the sidewalk.

Fifty feet later he skidded to halt. He toed the board, snapping it up into his hands. The attractive young reporter was waving her arms to get his attention. Bag lights flared to remove the harsh shadows of a high desert afternoon. The camera was rolling.

"Hello there, you a gambler?"

Solano nodded.

"Win or lose today?"

Solano grimaced. "A little of both."

"What's your poison, if you don't mind my asking?"

"Oh, sports book mostly."

The young reporter nodded. "You predict the game winners."

Solano wondered where this was going. "That I do."

"And you're good at it?"

"Yes, ma'am, I am . . . most of the time."

"Quite a hobby, I'd say."

"Not a hobby. It's how I make my living."

The young reporter grinned. She was elated; the perfect interview was standing right in front of her, already on camera.

"Sounds exciting. Tell me your name — ?"

"Mickey Solano."

"Well, Mr. Solano, we're here today from KNVR-TV to find out how the senatorial election is going to turn out."

"You a pollster?"

"The polling record is iffy this year, completely unreliable, so we thought we'd ask some serious players what they think. What's your guess?"

Solano's eyes darted this way and that. What had he gotten himself into? "Remind me who's running?"

"Ahh — that would be Senator Ives, the Democratic incumbent, running for his fourth term, and Conway Paxton, the Republican challenger."

"Oh yeah, I've heard of them." He could tell that he sounded like a jerk. He winced.

"So, got a prediction?" prompted the woman.

"I wouldn't lay down a bet" — he paused, actually starting to consider the problem — "but I guess I'd have to go with the senator. That guy Paxton, he's extreme, and he never held office. I'll take Ives." He paused again, mind whirling. "But Ives is old news. It will be close."

"Thank you, Mr. Solano."

"Sure thing."

Solano dropped his board on the sidewalk and legged away down the street. He zigged under the famous arch — *RENO, The Biggest Little City In The World* — and zagged toward a sporty white Range

Rover SUV.

The woman turned around to face the camera. "You heard it here, folks. Ives in a close one. This is Gigi Newhouse, KNVR's roving reporter, with our continuing not-so-scientific political analysis. Back to you."

▼

Reno occupied the far western corner of Nevada, separated from neighboring California by the High Sierra mountain range, a spectacular wall of granite. Its main connection to the Golden State was Interstate 80, following the steep course of the Truckee River, but the direct route to the resort towns of Lake Tahoe ran south via the Mount Rose Highway, State Route 431.

Solano maintained two homes, and on this afternoon he was escaping from the hot Nevada desert to the cooler lakeside two-thousand feet above the city and thirty-five miles farther west.

The road was a string of sharp curves and steep grades. As he guided his Range Rover through the rugged landscape, he took advantage of a lonely cell tower to make a hands-free telephone call.

"Yo, Cam, you there?"

"Mickey. How ya doin'? What's new?"

Cameron Hayes was a lawyer who doubled as Solano's financial adviser in a relationship that went back four years. When the bets started paying off, when the money started rolling in, Solano discovered he needed professional advice to organize a company and keep his taxes under control. Now he regarded the older man as family.

"Maybe a lot. Take a look at Sporting Insights, will you? Did a million dollars just show up there?"

"Sure, Mick, give me the account number and your secret code shit, Madge is gone for the day."

Solano rattled off the words and numbers.

"Okay, I'm taking notes, but I gotta ask, why me? Isn't Jake Quarles your accountant? Why aren't you calling him?"

"You're my lawyer, right? We have a contract."

"Of course we do. What's the problem? Did you steal something?"

"No, no. Lawyer-client privilege. Until I know more, I don't want anyone who might get subpoenaed to cite my concerns."

"He's gotta know, once he sees the books."

"That will be then, this is now."

"Okay, kid, call you back."

Solano continued up the grade, muttering to himself. When he left the switchbacks and entered the treeless alpine valley separating Mount Rose itself from the big ski resort on nearby Slide Mountain, another cell tower came into view, and his phone rang.

"Mickey? Here's the scoop — I couldn't get your stupid passwords past the operator, and I can't remember how much was in there yesterday, so I called Jake."

"Good Christ."

"Don't worry, I just asked for the total at your request, and yes, you've got a million more in your gaming account than you did twenty-four hours ago. Jake was pleased."

"No doubt."

"What's wrong, Mick? Why isn't this good news?"

"Oh, it is. It is."

"You don't sound like you're ready to party. Are you in trouble?"

"Nahh."

"Let me rephrase that — what kind of trouble are you in?"

Solano gripped the steering wheel tighter than needed as he wound into another set of Sierra switchbacks.

"Just a misunderstanding. I can handle it."

There was a moment of silence on the other end of the call. Solano could hear his lawyer's invisible deep frown. He hastened to reassure the man.

"Looks like I won a big bet. Wimbledon, can you believe? Just checking to make sure it paid off."

"A million bucks, Mickey. That's real money. Is it hot money? Don't push your luck."

"But that's what I always do."

Solano heard a weary sigh as Hayes rang off.

3

NEWS of the day.

On a large flat TV set, one of five in a dimly lit room, the call letters *K-N-V-R* zoomed into view riding on a stentorian musical fanfare. A wiggly line raced across the screen beneath the letters, leading the way to an aerial photo of Reno backed by the picturesque Sierra. A blocky logo appeared over the mountains and descended into the foreground:

Nevada News Night — NOW!

Standing behind a brushed metal desk on a glitzy set were KNVR's veteran news anchors: the well-groomed Maggie Morrison and Diego Ramirez, ready for petty crime, fires, and plenty of happy talk.

"It's *News Night,* folks," intoned Morrison with professional enthusiasm. "Welcome to the early edition. No fires big enough for TV coverage today in spite of our heat, no flaming car crashes, so this evening we're leading with an unsolved murder."

"That's right," continued Ramirez. "Last week, a man named Frank Osgood was found dead in his car in the Atlantis parking lot. Police originally concluded suicide."

Still photos of a drab Nissan Altima sedan appeared.

"But it wasn't?" queried Morrison, apparently shocked by the possibility of foul play. "I thought there was a note."

"There *was* a note *and* a gun. But forensic analysis — you know, that CSI stuff we all watch too much — found some of his hand-written documents, and the penmanship doesn't match up."

"Not his, Diego? Goodness, we have a mystery!"

"It's a big mystery, Mags. No suspects, no motive, no clues. Osgood was employed by Patriotic Decision Systems, the folks who make Nevada's electronic voting machines. Police are asking anyone with information to come forward."

A stock photo of Patriotic's Reno headquarters flashed onscreen.

"Voting machines? That brings us to politics," said Morrison, adroitly shifting into the next segment. "We're still catching our breath from the national election two years ago — but get ready, everybody — here we go again. Conway Paxton was in town today on the campaign trail. The primaries are over, he won a close race with his abrasive style, and now he's hot on Senator Ives' record."

Solano was tuning in the broadcast from his Incline Village home office on the north shore of Lake Tahoe. He wasn't focused on the news, however, because he was also watching four other screens: the never-ending *SportsCenter* and *MLB Tonight* shows alongside the *Bleacher Report* and *MarketWatch* websites. He was idly checking his net worth and mulling a betting strategy for tomorrow's games.

But the connection between Osgood, the murder victim, and the voting machine company caught his eye, scrambled his thoughts. He racked his brain to remember whether he had ever met the man. The software workforce in the Reno metro area was a tight little group, and most people involved had met each other at one time or another. But, he decided, Osgood was an unknown.

He was turning back to a story on Major League Soccer and the import of a new face arriving from the English Premier League when the newscast unreeled a video clip of Conway Paxton delivering a spirited campaign speech.

"Folks, it's good to be here in Reno. Good to be here in 'The Biggest Little City In The World'," said the candidate.

Solano noted Paxton's relative youth, his golf-shirt-style informality, his blue eyes, his square jaw, his quirky smile. He had to give the man credit, he was an attractive candidate. But the way he delivered the city's famous motto, surrounding it with audible quotes, put Solano off. He shuddered. Who is this guy?

Paxton thumped his lectern. "I'm here today to promise you two things — first, when I'm elected, Nevada won't be the forgotten state in Washington anymore. I'm going to shake up DC, get us westerners the respect we deserve. And second, I'm going to bring a business-man's expertise to the way we run our state and do away with the excessive regulations politicians find irresistible, regulations that are useless, regulations that have strangled our economy."

Solano clocked the standard right-wing boilerplate. He nodded to himself. If he were to bet the race, and he was starting to feel the itch, his money would still be on longtime Senator Maynard Ives.

He stared at the TV screens, osmotically absorbing the stream of information flowing toward him. He was hoping for inspiration, some hint on how to wriggle free of his troubles. Troubles, he was slowly grasping, that were likely to prove dangerous. But nothing hit him.

He waited through a barrage of commercials, vaguely curious to see if his man-in-the-street interview would run. Finally it did, and he heard himself predict an Ives victory. He was relieved to discover that the cute young reporter hadn't made him look like a total fool.

The stories then veered away to downtown parking problems. He gave up and gloomily pressed buttons, one after another, to turn off all five unhelpful displays.

▼

He wandered into the kitchen, selected a frosty bottle of Negra Modelo from the refrigerator, and strolled out onto his boat dock.

Tahoe days were long in late July, but mountains towering above the western shore had already cast the lake's vast expanse into shadow. The afternoon breeze had died out, and the surface was glassy. He slowly relaxed, and his natural optimism returned. Some-how, he silently vowed, he would find a way to overcome the threat posed by the management of his favorite gambling hall. He sank into a folding chair, popped the cap off his beer, and knocked back a slug.

Out on the lake, boats were few. Dusk was approaching, and vaca-tioners were leaving their watery pastimes in favor of bars and restau-rants. Solano's eyes were drawn to a Sea-Doo personal watercraft passing by, a hundred yards offshore. Its engine was sputtering.

The little craft alternately surged forward and drifted back, wallowing in its own wake. Then the engine quit entirely. The rider made several efforts to restart his tiny machine without success. He looked around, spotted Solano on his dock, and laboriously hand-paddled toward him.

Solano rose from his chair, put his beer aside, and gathered a coil of nylon rope with a plastic float attached. As the Sea-Doo neared, he tossed the float into the water. The rider leaned over, got a grip, and hauled himself to shore.

"Hello, Mickey," he said, as he dismounted and climbed onto the dock.

Solano was astonished. He performed a little head-slap and spread his arms. "Bill Gaffney, My God, is that you?"

"Been a while," said the man. Standing up he was tall and heavy. Long hair trailed out from under a camping hat. He was wearing a yellow life-vest over a pink T-shirt and plaid swimming trunks. Either a beard was starting, or he hadn't shaved in a week. "Thanks for the assist," he said. He was still wearing wraparound sunglasses at twilight.

"Haven't seen you in what — years," marveled Solano, being polite. "What happened to your ride?"

"Ran out of gas."

Solano gestured to an orange tank on the deck. "I've got a couple of gallons. How far is home?"

Gaffney nodded. He didn't seem to feel any urgency. "Nice place," he said, waving his arm toward Solano's expensive lakeside villa. "Owned it long?"

Solano shrugged. "Couple of years."

"Life is treating you well, old pal."

"Unh-huh," acknowledged Solano. He was proud of his stylish vacation home, and he was starting to wonder about his visitor. The man had always been eccentric.

"Gas . . ?"

Gaffney removed his glasses, studying Solano. "What I'd really like is a beer."

"Um, okay."

"And a bathroom. I need to take a leak."

Solano started back along the dock toward his house. "This way," he said.

4

GAFFNEY EMERGED from the bathroom, and Solano handed him a beer. They settled down on a redwood deck at the shoreline.

"Where are you staying?" inquired Solano, continuing to wonder about his chance encounter with an old friend he hadn't seen in years.

Gaffney pointed along the lake. "Down around the cove there. Renting a house for the month."

"Reno heat," agreed Solano with a nod.

The air at Lake Tahoe, by contrast, was rapidly cooling. Solano twisted a knob on a little table piled high with ceramic coals, pushed a button, and a warming propane fire blazed up.

Gaffney took note of his host. "You flying this big house all alone? Where's Lizzie?" he asked.

Solano shrugged uneasily over the resurrection of painful memories. "Lizzie doesn't live here anymore. LA, last I heard. We don't trade Christmas cards."

"What happened?"

"She was really upset when I started gambling. It took a while to get going, and she thought I was a disaster. And maybe she's religious, the moral angle. So she split. Married some real estate developer."

"Sorry, didn't mean to pry."

Gaffney took a long pull on his beer to cover his embarrassment. He regarded Solano through narrow eyes. "I left Patriotic. Quit last week."

Solano grinned. "The voting machine company. Voted with your feet, huh?"

"Ha-ha. Patriotic — man, what a hellhole. You're out of the software rat race, and maybe you've forgotten how weird it is."

Solano had not forgotten. He ground his teeth together. "I worked at HighScore with you, remember?"

"But you're a bigtime player now, a high roller, right? That's what they say."

Solano was irritated by Gaffney's apparent knowledge of his gaming activities. "Who says?"

"Dudes I talk to. It's no secret, man."

"So?"

"What's your take on the senate race?"

"The Nevada race . . . Ives and Paxton?"

"Yeah, who wins?"

Solano pursed his lips. "Ives," he declared.

"Put any money on it?"

"No. It's going to be close."

Gaffney pointed a finger. "Don't bet. You'll lose."

"Beg pardon?"

"Election fraud. Something's up with Patriotic." Gaffney's head bobbed vigorously. "Broheims around the campaign, they're going to steal our senate seat."

Solano thought this idea was impossible, a ridiculous notion. "Oh? Which campaign is that?"

Gaffney had his suspicions, but no evidence, and he knew that undercut his claims. "Maybe the Russians are involved," he said.

Solano shifted uncomfortably in his chair. His former colleague seemed to have drifted over the edge. "That sounds a little like one of those conspiracy theories."

"No theory, pal." Gaffney was adamant. "Far out shit is going on all the time. The Man In Charge — does He have a plan? Or does He just roll the dice? Either way, a lot of the results are beyond human imagination."

"Really. And, you know, the last time we talked I thought you were reasonably sane," said Solano, opting for a lighthearted tone. But even as he spoke he noticed that, underneath the casual pose, his visitor was actually bothered by something.

Gaffney raised his eyebrows. "You hear about Frank?"

"The dead guy? Osgood? I saw an item on the news."

"Once is happenstance —he was busy writing sabotage code for Patriotic's machines."

"Huh?"

"Twice is coincidence — he had a change of heart. Maybe that's what got him killed."

"Went to the cops?"

"No, asked for a big raise . . . that could be seen as a threat."

"Murdered to save a dollar? What a joke."

"No joke, my friend. I was working on the same stuff. The wrapper, basically."

"So, how will whoever-they-are do their frauding? Nevada requires a paper trail."

Gaffney nervously surveyed the lakefront, checking for eavesdroppers. "Who knows how it works? I just know the code exists, and Frank's dead."

"Christ, Bill, what's eating you?" asked Solano, skeptically aware of Gaffney's anxiety, and completely unconvinced by the story he was hearing.

"Everything, man. Life is plotting against us. In the store, you're always in the longest line. You can't ever win the lottery. And watch yourself — *pow!* — when the meteor hits."

With that, Gaffney drained his beer, stood, and headed off down the dock. Halfway along he called a parting remark over his shoulder: "Three times is enemy action — if I'm next, Mick, then you'll know what I'm talking about."

"Gas in the can, there," reminded Solano.

Gaffney waved and, ignoring the offer, slipped aboard his Sea-Doo. It started right up.

5

SOLANO AMBLED out to the end of his dock to watch Gaffney motor away down the lake. The Sea-Doo's engine was running smoothly, and soon it was out of view in the failing light.

He walked slowly back to his house. Above, stars were coming out. Gray half-light on the western shore promised to bring a silvery moon over the mountains in an hour or two.

His thoughts turned to baseball. What was the worst team in either league? The Devil Rays? — Twins? — how about those hopeless Diamondbacks? But wait, hang on, the Snakes had an arm in Greinke, a guy who could pitch, a guy who won some games in spite of his mediocre teammates.

He was just making up his mind to lose the Silverlode's money on the Rays when —

. . . *boo-boo-boom.* . .

— he heard a faint rumble, like distant thunder. A reddish glow appeared on the windows of his house. He spun around to look.

"Damn."

Half a mile away on the lakefront, flames were leaping into the treetops where a house was burning. In less than a minute, the wail of sirens floated across the water, a welcome sign that the Incline Village Fire Department was on the job. Not my problem, Solano decided. He downed the rest of his beer and marched into his office.

He spent a half hour studying the week's baseball results, confirming his opinion of the pathetic Rays. But what if a bet on those bozos looked suspicious? He was unaccustomed to doubt, and to shake it off he paced back and forth in front of his TV screens, pondering the matter. Finally he checked the online spread, and to his relief it was big enough to make a long-shot play look respectable. So be it.

He sat down and scribbled some notes. But then, half-finished, he dropped his pencil and went back outside. That damn fire. Standing on his deck he could still see emergency lights flashing and smoke rising, but the lurid tongues of flame were gone.

Gaffney had motored off in that direction, he remembered. And the man had been full of crazy plots and conspiracies. You don't suppose . . ?

▼

Well, crap. Second thoughts about Gaffney's claims propelled Solano into his Range Rover and out onto Tahoe Boulevard. He cruised slowly along southward, scanning the area for signs of the disaster, but the fire was invisible, and any response vehicles were hidden behind houses and trees. He was mumbling to himself. After an uncertain half mile or so, he made a wild guess at the probable location and turned toward the lake on Pine Nut Drive. Nearing the shore, his guess was rewarded by a carnival's worth of flashing lights and a street full of fire trucks, police cars, and emergency vehicles.

He parked, got out, and hiked to the scene, stepping over a tangle of fire hoses and skirting the water that was all over the pavement, a sloppy byproduct of the fire department's efforts. The fire was out, and the house in question was now little more than a concrete foundation. Only a few sticks, some crumbled drywall, and a brick fireplace still stood among the ashes.

Firemen were wrapping up their equipment. Solano watched a couple of police officers girdle the property with *POLICE LINE DO NOT CROSS* tape. He also observed their attempt to calm a distraught older woman who was gesticulating wildly at the ruins. After a moment she seemed to sag under the weight of the event. She trudged across the street to a Jaguar sedan where Solano intercepted her.

"Your house?"

"What?"

The woman blinked, obviously shaken and confused. An arm rose and waved dismissively at the mess. "Oh, yes. Property yesterday, numbers in a bank account tomorrow . . . or next year, more likely, before the insurance pays off."

"Sorry about your loss. Still got your car, I see. That's something."

The woman glanced at her fancy automobile. "It's a nice car, isn't it?"

"Got a place to stay?"

The woman seemed to wake up. "Oh, I don't live here, young man. It's one of my rentals. Was, anyway."

Solano was taken aback. "Oh. Too bad, but could be worse, huh?"

"One of the neighbors told me the place exploded. Apparently my renter left the gas on."

"Renter?" Solano's mind was racing. "Was it a guy named Gaffney?"

"Why yes. You knew him?"

"A friend."

"Well, your friend is dead, I'm afraid. They wanted me to identify the body." She laughed nervously. "What body?"

Solano nodded goodnight and moved on to the police presence.

"I'm a neighbor" — he tilted his head toward the north end of the lake — "the landlady told me you found a body."

The senior cop scowled at the intruding looky-loo and pointed to the still-smoldering foundation. "In the kitchen over there. Those metal panels used to be a stove."

"It could be a friend of mine."

The cop was suddenly interested. "Want to look? Watch out for nails." He motioned Solano onto the concrete pad and led the way to a rusted-out sink hanging from bent-over water pipes. Human remains were visible in the ashes nearby. A skull, some long bones, a belt buckle, the melted rubber soles from a pair of shoes.

Solano stared dumbly at the shocking bits and pieces.

"How about it? Can you make an ID?" The cop was hoping to tie a knot on the evening.

"Are you kidding?"

"No, huh? Well shit — pardon me — neither could the old lady."

6

THE SILVERLODE Sports Book looked like a cross between the New York Stock Exchange and NASA Mission Control. A dozen live athletic events were simultaneously running on huge TV screens arrayed across the back wall of a dimly lit room. A hundred other pending events, together with the odds, the spreads, and the money lines, were listed in bright glowing colors on a side wall, like the arrival displays in the nation's airports. Bettors sat in fifteen rows of private seats, each with its own TV screen and microphone.

Solano strolled up to a kiosk under the video circus and conveyed a series of bets to the book manager, Eric Sparling, a spare man a generation older than his superstar customer.

"Come on, Mickey, the Rays? The Twins? Big bucks on both? This is not like you. Not like the Solano I know. What gives?"

Solano made a little bow, admitting some embarrassment. "I've got a hunch, Sparkles. Looking for long shots to come in."

"Christ on an inside straight — why not bet the sun won't rise?"

"I would, but you don't list the spread."

Sparling threw up his hands and registered the bets. "Lock up your guns, throw away your kitchen knives. When the bad news comes in, I don't want to hear any sad stories."

"Take it easy. I've got a cushion. Things are going my way."

"Were, you mean." Sparling shook his head. "This is pathetic."

Solano grinned and gave the manager an affectionate nudge. "I know what I'm doing — but this is not a tip, old man."

"That's funny, Mickey. You're hysterical."

On his way out of the building, Solano passed by the house café where a TV set was screening the news. Senator Maynard Ives was on camera charging up his followers at a Las Vegas rally.

"Trying to get rid of me?" he asked rhetorically. The crowd roared its loyalty. "Send me back to Washington instead — that's where I can make a difference for Nevada, bring social justice to all of our citizens, stop the big corporations and special interests from destroying our land."

Then it was challenger Paxton's turn to rail about modern life's unfair restrictions on life, liberty, and the pursuit of happiness.

Solano was revolted by both candidates, but he couldn't have put his feelings into words. Something about the sappy appeals to voter prejudice, the ridiculous simplification of tough issues, the bold promises that would never grind their way through Congress, the condescending tone. He let out a disgusted sigh.

He was turning away when the scene shifted back into the KNVR studio, and Gigi Newhouse appeared to arbitrate the contest.

"Well, there you have it folks. It's a vigorous campaign, short on facts, maybe, but long on passion. Looks like Senator Ives has a real challenge on his hands — for the first time in his long career."

The political sparring caused Solano to reconsider Gaffney's paranoid notions. An idea started to tickle his brain. He stepped outside, moved under an awning at the entrance to a nearby pawn shop, and placed a call to KNVR. A dozen key presses led him past the telephone robot to a real live receptionist.

"Hello? Gigi Newhouse, please."

Pause.

"My name is Mickey Solano."

Pause.

"Right, understood. She's busy. We're all busy. Listen, I have a tip for her."

Pause.

"It's a real tip. She'll be glad to get it."

Pause.

"Tell her it's from the guy she interviewed on the street outside the Silverlode." He repeated his name, and the receptionist promised to relay the message.

Solano walked the block and a half to his Range Rover at a thoughtful pace. His longboard stayed tucked under an arm. He was unlocking the car door when his phone rang.

"This is Solano . . . whoa, Miss Newhouse, hey there, thanks for calling back."

▼

The Turquoise Tavern, a low-key eatery on West 2nd Street, was a study in oak. Oak bar, oak chairs, oak-paneled walls, oak blades on the old-fashioned ceiling fans. The clientele was old Reno, and it spanned the range from saddle-sore cowboys in work shirts to bankers in their summer suits. The soft interior lighting gave way at the door to bright sunshine on a concrete plaza filled with stainless steel tables under festive umbrellas.

Solano was slouching there with a pint of locally-brewed beer when Gigi Newhouse strode up behind him.

"Well, if it isn't the skateboard gambler. Got a seat for me?"

Solano bounced to his feet, startled by her stealthy arrival. The KNVR reporter wasn't dressed for camera, and instead of her corporate threads she was wearing a lime-green T-shirt and Daisy Duke cutoff jeans. She had a baseball cap pulled down over her auburn hair. He maneuvered a chair into position.

"Thanks for meeting me."

Newhouse sat. They looked at each other.

"Oh no," she said, pointing at his dark blue cap and the ornate red capital *B* embroidered above the bill. Solano pointed back at the cap she herself was wearing, with its interlaced *N* and *Y*.

"The Yankees?" he growled with good-natured contempt, "How could anyone outside the Bronx root for those overpaid, overhyped, over-the-hill has-beens?"

"Oh? You prefer the Red Sox, the most racist club in the most racist city in America?"

They both laughed.

Solano ordered another beer and Newhouse ordered a margarita.

"So," she said, "what's the tip? I could use one."

Solano leaned forward, knitted his hands together. "Election fraud. The senate race? Nevada's voting machines are made right here in town by Patriotic Decision Systems. Some of those machines are going to be rigged."

Newhouse sipped her drink. "That's a pretty big tip. Who would do it? How would they do it?"

Solano shook his head. "I have no idea. We need to smoke these guys out. You're in position, on TV and all, to do just that."

Newhouse made a face. "I can't actually claim fraud on the air without some evidence, a reliable source."

"I'm reliable. Use Osgood's murder. The guy worked for Patriotic, and I think he was hit — to cover somebody's tracks."

"Wow," she said.

"There's more. An old friend of mine just showed up out of the blue. He worked for Patriotic too, until last week. He told me Osgood was writing *sabotage code."*

"Really . . ." She was grinning, amused by the far-out conspiracy theory.

Solano registered her skepticism. It annoyed him. "Really. This is really real. And — now get this — my friend's house burned down last night."

"What does that prove? Careless with matches?"

"He was inside when it blew up. He's dead."

Newhouse downed her margarita and ordered another one. "I need names, facts."

"You already reported on Osgood. My friend's name is Bill Gaffney. Connect the dots. This is your chance to, to, I dunno — do some good."

"Oh please. I'm not Woodward and Bernstein."

Solano studied her. He frowned. "So, a good story is just some tar on the road to a better job?" He indicated her cap. "New York, here I come?"

"Ooh, the man's a hitter. Ground rule double." She lifted a contradictory finger. "Ambition is a good thing."

"Just trying to fire you up, no offense."

"Tell you what, coach — I'll check with my editor. Not sure he'll okay a story like this."

Solano nodded appreciatively. "I'm betting he will."

7

WALTER BASCOMB, a round little man of forty or so, resigned from the political consulting firm of Bascomb, Chambers, and Rivkin, a staunch Republican outfit run by his father, in order to work more directly on conservative causes for the wealthy industrialist Lloyd Snell, a passionate right-wing activist.

Today he flew to Reno from his office in Los Angeles and then drove forty miles through the Sierra to Snell's Northern California vacation home on the slopes of Mount Pluto, tucked into the trees edging the Northstar-at-Tahoe ski resort.

He needed a stiff drink after the taxing trip, and Snell's domestic staff was happy to supply it.

"Excellent scotch, boss. Hits the spot."

He wiped his mouth and opened his briefcase.

"Here's what we've got going on . . ."

Snell, a stately gentleman just entering his seventies, was tall and thin and patrician. He reached out and gently closed the briefcase.

"We'll get to that, Wally. Numbers, poll results, all important. But first — what about our own proactive initiatives? Eh? Any news?"

Bascomb looked troubled. He cast his eyes around the room. "No cameras, right? Nobody recording us?"

"Good Lord no. At least we learned *something* of value from that moron Nixon, didn't we?"

"I guess." Bascomb patted his pockets, pulled out a crumpled sheet of paper, looked it over. "I have been informed" — he stuffed the sheet back in his jacket — "that all traces have been wiped."

"Wiped? Meaning?"

Bascomb was bouncing uncomfortably on the balls of his feet. "Meaning . . . I don't know. Our contractor isn't exactly my idea of a regular businessman or professional spy. When I questioned him, he was a bit . . . intimidating. He looked capable of anything."

"Anything . . ?"

Bascomb nervously adjusted a pair of horn-rimmed glasses.

"Anything at all."

Snell nodded. "Sounds melodramatic, but don't fret, we're not involved. It's an arms-length transaction."

"Right, but we're skating on thin ice. Say our plan goes into operation, and we manage to exert some influence on the election — our resources are limited. We have yet to suborn an inspector for the election commission, either in Vegas or Reno. Understand? Paxton has to make it close to make our work pay off."

"I do understand. We need something else. Something to close those poll numbers."

Bascomb was relieved to hear Snell's reaction, having given the matter some thought on his drive through the mountains.

"How about a scandal?"

"Explain — Ives, damn the man, is a model citizen."

"How do we know? How does anyone else? Suppose we hire a woman who will claim she is Ives' paid escort. We get her standing up beside the guy at his next rally, and then she comes forward."

"The honeypot angle. Wally, you clever boy. But we have to make sure the idea will play on TV."

"That's the easy part — the networks will go crazy. Virtuous husband exposed! Hypocrisy of the powerful! Sexual harassment!"

"Who's the woman?" A sly smile formed on Snell's lips. "Should I get to know her?"

"Whoa, good joke. Let me talk to our contractor, see if he has a candidate in mind."

Snell chuckled. "There's only one problem — Ives really *is* a virtuous husband. He wouldn't do it."

Bascomb grinned. "We don't care, boss. We just want to hear him deny it."

8

IT TOOK MORE than a week and twenty bad bets, but Solano managed to gamble away a million dollars that didn't belong to him. The book manager was sympathetic. He couldn't understand why his favorite bettor didn't need a lot of cheering up.

"Bad week, Mickey. I warned you."

"Don't worry about it, Sparkles." He let out a deep and painful sigh. "I'll climb out of the hole."

"Sure you will — just stay away from these stupid long shots."

Sparling looked up to see Ed Barber approaching. The man was grinning from ear to ear.

"Talk to you, Mick, take care of yourself." He edged away to his little kiosk and busied himself sorting receipts.

"Mickey! Mickey Solano, how are you?" boomed the casino big-wig. He smacked Solano on the shoulder and shook his hand with congratulatory gusto.

Solano cringed. "We're square, Mr. Barber. For the first and only time in my life — I just lost an actual fortune."

"As we agreed . . ."

"Yeah, whew! Do you know how tough that is?" He wiped an imaginary layer of sweat off his brow. "Thank God it was your money."

Barber's smile faded. "Well, you didn't quite lose the whole thing. One of your ridiculous long shots paid off, I hear."

"Yeah, the Padres worst pitcher shut out the Nats yesterday. I thought you were going to twist the outcome if it came to that."

"Not necessary in this case. What's the payoff? Fifty-K? Take it with our blessing. Your fee."

"I'm not looking for any fee."

"Don't be silly, you earned it. And we'll be doing this waltz again. Look for another drop in about two weeks."

"Oh no, that's it, I'm out."

Barber stood up straighter, raised his chin aggressively. "What was that? Think, Mickey. You work for us now."

"No, I sure as hell don't."

"That's no way to talk. Don't be an ass. You walk away? Then you lose a *lot* of bets."

"How? I'll sleep better."

"Not with Dick Worden on your case. He's got a mean streak." Barber worked up a smile to soften the threat. "But here's an even better idea — we *list* you in the Griffin Book, tell the world what a terrible thief you are. Set you up for the bum's rush in every casino statewide."

Solano swallowed hard. Such measures would likely destroy his livelihood.

"Okay, Mr. Barber," he mumbled. He could hardly talk. "But you have to space it out. No more than two-hundred-K a whack."

Barber slapped Solano on the back. "That's my boy. Two-hundred-K it is. Max."

AUGUST

9

THE NEWS at noon.

KNVR was leading its show with Senator Ives at a Reno rally. *"Con*-way *Pax*-ton," he mocked, voice dripping with contempt. "That man, forget the name and remember the shame. He's never held office. He's got plans to sell the state to the highest bidder. So I say, don't let that Con-man Piss-on you, the voters of Nevada. You deserve a real senator, a man with the experience to lead this state through the pitfalls in Congress."

Ives continued to rant, but the sound of his voice was cut off as his image repositioned itself on a grid of video screens behind Diego Ramirez, the news anchor.

"Well, you heard it. The senator got a little carried away there. With language like that, he must be worried. Paxton trails in all the polls, but he's not going away."

Maggie Morrison, Ramirez' on-air partner, walked into the shot. "No, Diego, he's not. And now we have what could be the makings of a scandal. Look at these clips from Ives' recent rallies . . ."

The view cut to shots of Ives on various podiums, flanked by aides and none other than the Silverlode's Jenny Penny. The camera angles and telephoto lenses clearly demonstrated her presence here and there in the background and along the sidelines.

It was hard to tell if she was part of the senator's entourage or just a bystander, but KNVR wasn't in a mood to express any doubts.

"The woman you see onstage there is Jennifer Penrose," said Morrison. "She claims that she was sexually abused by the senator after he hired her as his paid companion."

Jenny Penny stood under the Reno Arch downtown and reiterated her complaint for Gigi Newhouse and the KNVR news team in a dramatic close-up.

"Yes, it's true," she lamented, "the senator hired me to accompany him on his travels around the state. What an opportunity for one of his fans! I was expected to remain discreetly in the background, which I was happy to do, but I was not prepared for sexual assault. Everyone thinks they know him. I saw a different man."

Back in the studio, Ramirez shook his head in wonderment. "Quite a shock, I'd say. Until now, the senator has had the reputation of a solid family man."

Morrison adopted a sympathetic expression. "How does his wife feel?"

"We can only speculate about her, Margaret, but here's the man himself, what does he say?"

Now Ives took over the screen to deny everything. His face was red with righteous anger, and his campaign manager hastened to offer a calmer view:

"This is a complete and utter fabrication. Nevada knows their senior senator as an upright gentleman with nothing but the highest moral standards. Neither he nor anyone on his campaign hired this woman for any purpose whatsoever."

Ramirez grinned. "I guess that's what I'd say too, if I got caught with my pants down."

"Not funny, Diego," objected Morrison. "This is a serious charge. Let's take a look at Paxton's reaction . . ."

Conway Paxton took a low-key approach, as if saddened by developments. "I guess it's too much to ask my opponent and his team of useless bureaucrats to tell the truth. That's what you get from an old man, a has-been from another age when this kind of ugly behavior went unnoticed and unreported. Well, no longer, folks."

Morrison picked up the cue. "Sad, isn't it? You'd think by now everyone, especially public servants, would have learned."

Ramirez shook his head. "Hey, senator, remember *I Love Lucy?* Big show in your day — well, sir — you got some *splainin'* to do!"

10

DICK WORDEN knocked on Ed Barber's corner office door on the second floor of the Silverlode Casino and Sports Book. He waited a beat, then pushed the door open.

"Got a guy here, Ed, wants to see you."

Barber raised his eyebrows, mildly surprised by the unscheduled intrusion. "What's his business?"

Another man squeezed past Worden and advanced to Barber's desk. He opened his wallet to show the executive an ID.

"Luke Voss, Mr. Barber. Nevada Gaming Control Board."

If Barber was unnerved by the announcement, he smoothly avoided showing it. "Have a seat," he said.

Voss, a cool customer in his thirties, casually lowered himself onto the only available chair and leaned back like he owned the place.

"Any idea why I'm here today, Mr. Barber?"

Barber smiled. He recognized and appreciated the cop's conscious effort to overcome his relative youth, to look comfortably authoritative, to be the man in charge.

"Not a clue. We're in compliance with all the regs. No outstanding customer complaints I'm aware of."

"What's your bet?" probed Voss.

Barber's smile evaporated. "It may surprise you to learn — Mister Voss, is it? — I'm not a betting man."

Voss inclined his head to acknowledge being rude. He dug into the case slung over his shoulder and withdrew a sheaf of papers.

"Sorry, I don't mean to be obscure. We're interested in the Silverlode's financial condition. Your company does business overseas. And you have quite a lot of money in offshore accounts as a result."

"Yes we do."

"The Board has noticed that a large sum on deposit in the Cayman Islands recently disappeared. A million dollars. We'd like to know where it went. Can you tell us?"

Barber looked wounded. "How do you have knowledge of our financial arrangements in another country where your agency has zero jurisdiction?"

Voss opened his arms to embrace the always mysterious world of law enforcement. "Some of our info comes from your corporate tax filings here in Nevada. They're subject to scrutiny, and we scrutinize. That's all I can tell you about our investigative techniques, I'm afraid."

Barber drummed his fingers on his desk. "You think we're bringing money into the country illegally, tax-free, is that it?"

"Good guess. Yup, we are concerned."

"We would never do that."

"I wish I could take you at your word, Mr. Barber, but we need to be convinced by facts." Voss withdrew a legal document from his case. "I have here a subpoena — you need to show us your books."

Voss attempted to hand the document to Barber, who made no effort to receive it. After an awkward moment he dropped it on Barber's desk with a shrug.

"Mr. Worden, here, will witness that you have been served."

Barber's manner hardened. "You probably know this, but I'll tell you anyway. The Silverlode is a private company. It's financial dealings are proprietary. And to keep it that way, we maintain an excellent legal staff. They're pretty good at their trade, and will no doubt advise us to resist your order in court."

He motioned to Worden. "Dick, would you be so kind? Escort the gentleman out."

▼

Voss's Gaming Board vehicle was an old and unmarked Dodge Charger, parked a block from the Silverlode. As he turned the corner on West 4th Street, he observed a raggedy man leaning into the passenger side front window. He was lifting a leather camera case into view.

"Hey!"

Voss broke into a run. Upon reaching the car he spotted shards of glass all over the sidewalk. The man dropped his prize back inside and stood away. He was wearing a grimy jumpsuit. His dark hair was long, unwashed, and uncombed.

"Dude! What the fuck!" growled Voss.

The man was nervous and agitated. On closer inspection it was obvious he hadn't shaved or taken a shower in some time. He indicated the open car window and broken glass on the ground with a grease-stained hand.

"I was just noticing that you had yourself a break-in here, and I was making sure nothing got taken," he said.

Voss wasn't large or imposing, but he had a good cop's instinctive self-confidence. He grabbed a fistful of the man's jumpsuit and jerked him close. "You picked the wrong car, asshole."

"I didn't do nothing. I was just trying to help. Shouldn't leave things in plain sight like that. Cameras, expensive things."

"Guess what, you scrote — I'm a cop. Who the hell are you?"

"Just walking by, that's all."

"Show me some ID. Got a drivers license?"

"Sure I do."

Voss thrust him away. "Show me."

The man took a tentative step backwards.

"Make another move and your happy feet will be dancing in jail."

The man halted, fished around in his jumpsuit, and produced his wallet. He held up his drivers license. Voss inspected it.

"Wilbur Rollins Guyette. Is that your name?"

The man nodded, trying to figure the depths of his legal peril. "Folks call me Rolly."

"Okay, there, Rolly — this your present address?"

"Oh no. That's last year. I moved on."

"I'll bet. Got a job?"

"Course I do. Cleaning out my friend's store down on Liberty."

"You're a janitor?"

"Sometimes I fix cars. Not new ones, like yours here, but they run good."

"You got a car?"

"Yep. A Caddy. Nice one too."

"Here's the deal, Rolly, you pathetic excuse for I-don't-know-what. You are going to work hard and bring me the price of my window — in cash."

"I can't afford that. Got to eat, man."

"Try my generous installment plan. Half this week, half in one month. Pay up or we garnish your wages and pull you in for vandalism and theft."

The man suddenly turned and bolted.

"My job? Ha-ha-ha, I just quit, ha-ha-ha!"

Voss started off in pursuit, then thought better of the idea. He watched the vandal leg it around the 3rd Street corner with a shake of his head.

"Run, you sad piece of shit."

11

SOLANO WAS WORKING in his home office on Lake Tahoe, watching re-runs of pre-season National Football League games. He was looking for clues to predict results when the teams started clashing for real, and when he would be laying down heavy bets. He hadn't bothered to dress yet, although it was almost noon.

The doorbell rang.

He switched channels to his surveillance camera feed. Standing on the flagstones outside, fidgeting with a pocketful of car keys, he saw a guy who looked like he could be his brother, if he had a brother. Not too tall, wiry, regular features, just about the same age. Who the hell?

He slipped into a terrycloth bathrobe, toed his feet into a pair of flip-flops, and padded away to his front door. He pressed a button on an intercom.

"Who is it?"

"Mr. Solano? It's Luke Voss. Nevada Gaming Control Board."

"Trixie, unlock the front door," commanded Solano, activating his artificially intelligent and geek-certified virtual servant.

"Unlocking Door One. Warning — your lakeside home is now insecure," piped the audiobot.

"Yeah, I know."

Solano opened the door and stepped out. Voss held up his badge.

"Uh-oh," said Solano, scanning the ID. "What's the problem?"

"Not sure there is one. We're curious about the Silverlode. We know you've done business there, won a lot of money."

"True." Solano looked past the officer to see what his ride looked like. "You're a long way from home, way up here."

"My day off. Thought I'd cruise the lake."

"Unh-huh. Am I under arrest or something?"

"This is just a knock-and-talk. Can I come in?"

All of Solano's danger detectors were vibrating. "Is that necessary?"

He indicated a teak table and chairs on a little patio beside the door. "It's nice out here."

Voss didn't move. He folded his arms. "We looked at your receipts. Very unusual. You're a big winner, and now suddenly, a big loser. And we got to wondering, how do you do it?"

"I bet on sporting events."

"What kind of events?"

"Anything — you name it — baseball, football, soccer, chickens crapping in a box."

"Really. Most gamblers lose. But not you, until recently. And you do this without any help from the kindly casino staff."

"You're a Board enforcer, right? So you must know — sports betting is a skill. There is no house edge. They take my fee — the vig — and I take my winnings. Or losses, now and then."

"And all this without cheating Nevada and Uncle Sam?"

Solano felt a steely calm come over him now that he understood he was being targeted for some offense.

"Listen, officer — I've got an excellent accountant who keeps excellent records. Never drops a penny, finds all the little tax breaks coming to me. I've also got a real good lawyer. Talk to them, they'll be glad to explain my life to you."

"Sure you're not cooperating with the Silverlode? Helping bring some of their offshore money home?"

Solano's skin went cold. Somehow, the State of Nevada was onto his deal with the devil. He cursed inwardly.

"What I do is actual work. Honest work. I study the stats, check the scores. Watch all those damn sports shows on TV. Research, okay? Then I digest the information — lay a bet — I just know how to play."

Voss nodded skeptically. "Wish I did. See you around, Solano. We'll be talking again."

The lawman walked back to his car, and drove away with a cheery wave.

▼

Solano thought about the odd encounter while he showered and dressed. It was not possible to tell the truth. Not about the Silverlode's offshore money, and not about his honest work. He did look at the stats, he did check the scores, and he did watch the sports shows, but there was more to the story.

He carried a cup of instant coffee back into his home office, flipped on his TV screens, and went back to work. But the pressure was cooking him. The Silverlode wanted Cayman money laundered. The Gaming Control Board either wanted him indicted, or more likely, he suspected, they were angling for voluntary testimony that would incriminate the Silverlode management. He worried that any such testimony could lead to an untimely death.

He turned all five TV monitors off and paced around the room, grumbling and mumbling. Then, forcing himself to focus, he turned them all back on. He stared at *SportsCenter*. The chatterheads were discussing the New England Patriots, the legendary Tom Brady's possible past concussions, his chances of playing in another Super Bowl.

"A little early in the year for this, don't you think?" he groused aloud.

He punched buttons to kill all five screens yet again.

"You morons, I will take the points against anyone you recommend."

He stood up and wandered out onto his dock. He peered into the distance, down along the shoreline to where his programmer friend's rented house once stood. Solano felt the pressure he was under like a physical weight. But at least he was still alive, whereas poor Bill Gaffney . . .

12

BY MIDAFTERNOON Solano was too restless to continue working. To escape from the burden of his legal worries, he drove down the lake to the site of Gaffney's house fire. There he parked, got out, and crossed the street to the burned-out residence. The yellow police tape was sagging. Charred planks that once defined the floor plan were crumbling. The police presence was no more.

He stepped onto the concrete pad and made a little tour of the blackened foundation. He was wondering about his late friend, about the guy's obsession with Patriotic Decision Systems, about the claim that Frank Osgood, a programmer Solano had never heard of, was working on some kind of election fraud. It was hard to believe.

Apparently nobody had yet been hired to clean up the mess. His foot touched a blackened lump, knocking ashes off. It glistened in the afternoon light. He bent to pick it up and discovered the melted remains of a what might once have been a small tablet computer. Gaffney's? Probably.

Pasted to the underside, only partly singed, was a sticker. He wiped the grime off. Some of the text was still readable: *Prop . . . P . . . riotic . . . Dec . . . Sys . . .*

He whistled through his teeth. While he was handling it, the warped case cracked open. Computer chips fell out, bouncing on the concrete. They looked like bits of blackened popcorn. Their computing days were over.

Beep!

The sound of an elegant car horn turned him around. Across the street a silver Lexus SUV had pulled up behind his Range Rover. Gigi Newhouse was standing by the driver's door, hand on the horn. She waved. Solano waved back.

By the time he picked his way back to the street, Newhouse had a professional digital camera ready and was photographing the site.

"Miss Newhouse . . ."

"It's Gigi."

"What are you doing here?" he wondered. He couldn't help noticing a pair of long tan legs beneath her Daisy Duke cut-offs.

"Looking for evidence. My tipster — that's you, mister — didn't supply any, so I thought I'd take a look at the scene of the crime. If, in fact, it is the scene of any crime."

"There's not much to see."

"Too bad. I tried calling your house and then thought, the only reality to your fanciful ideas about voter fraud was this burned-out building, and look who's here."

"Yeah, I'm hooked."

"Move over, I need video coverage." She pushed him to one side, pressed the record button on her camera, and made a hi-res panorama of the site.

"What's the idea?"

"B-roll."

"You going to do a story on the air?"

"Maybe. I'm pushing for one."

"About time."

She cocked her head, smiled coyly, and made a show of looking him over. "I didn't know you were such a high roller when I interviewed you outside the Silverlode. Or that you used to write computer code for HighScore, that video slot machine company in town."

"You googled me."

"The station has excellent search tools. So tell me, in between bets, you dig up any evidence to justify your accusations?"

He showed her the tablet computer case, with the partially legible sticker.

"That? That is one thin slice of salami."

He nodded.

She took a close-up photo.

▼

Solano led Newhouse out to the end of his dock. He twisted the tops off a couple of beers and handed her one.

"So this is where you live?" she said, openly gawking.

"Part time."

"Nice work if you can get it. Big windows. Look at all that glass."

"Shouldn't you be in the studio, getting ready for showtime or something?"

She clinked the neck of her bottle against his. "Here's to field research."

Solano regarded her thoughtfully. She was pretty. She was smart. She was also kind of antsy, he decided. He had never met anyone like her. "You're not happy at KNVR, and you're not really headed for New York. What's the move? San Francisco? Seattle?"

She grinned as if sharing a secret. "Seattle would be nice."

"And my crazy tale, you're here to buy a ticket?"

"That's the cover story anyway." Her eyes were sparkling.

Solano found himself calculating a trajectory for the evening. She was definitely flirting.

"Tell you what," he said, making up his mind. "The sun over there is just about to drop behind the mountain."

"Unh-huh."

"Ever ride on a jet ski?"

"Nope."

He pointed across the northern arm of the lake toward the California shore. "We could zip over to the Borderline. Great steaks, pasta, margaritas."

"Will I get wet?"

"They've got a big stone fireplace. You won't melt."

"Mmm . . ."

Ten minutes later Newhouse was mounted up behind Solano on his Yamaha WaveRunner, roaring across the lake. At first the water was calm and smooth. But out away from shore the surface became choppy.

"Ooh, ooh, ooh," groaned Newhouse.

"Should I slow down?" asked Solano.

"Noooo!" she shouted.

A big ski boat crossed ahead of them, producing an enormous wake. Solano plowed right through it, causing his tiny Yamaha to buck like a horse.

"Whoooee," sang out Newhouse. "It's Mickey, right? That's what they call you?"

He nodded.

▼

At the Borderline in August, loose shirts and flip-flops counted as formal dress. Dinner on the lakeside deck, following tequila shots in front of the restaurant's spectacular fireplace, was long and slow and relaxed. Gazpacho and a steak for Solano. A pistachio-encrusted chicken breast for Newhouse. Large glasses of expensive wine for both. She seemed to forget all about her role on TV once the waiter stopped gushing over meeting her, and they both retailed embarrassing anecdotes.

"So there I was," said Newhouse, "covering that winter flood down by the airport, and I fell in the mud. On camera, on the air."

"Whoa."

"My worst moment. Except Diego loved it. He re-ran my splat like thirty times for a week."

"My first job at HighScore was orchestrating some video clips for *Doomsday Champions.*" said Solano, cringing at the thought. "I allocated memory repeatedly inside a loop, and de-allocated it outside when the loop finished."

Newhouse looked blank.

Solano squirmed. "It produced a horrendous memory leak."

Newhouse crossed her eyes. "Wow. A leak. Stupid, huh?"

"Box-of-rocks stupid. My manager was furious. I was almost fired."

Newhouse forked up the last of her salad. "But you don't write code anymore."

"I don't miss it. Long hours, hard work, all detail."

"Now you gamble. You win. Doesn't that involve work?"

"See? That's my secret," he confessed. "While I was writing all those damn random number generators — that's how you program chance in a modern video slot — I discovered that I have this sixth sense."

Newhouse elevated her eyebrows to politely express the natural doubts of any sane person. *"What?"*

"I started predicting the sequences. Probabilities — I can sense them. No thinking required."

Newhouse smiled the way parents indulge a favored child. "That's absurd. You're teasing me."

"No I'm not," he avowed. "And, hey" — he rubbed two fingers together — "I've got some money to prove it."

"Good point and a valid one," she conceded. "You sense *probabilities*. That's it? That's your system?"

"That's it."

"I'm not the butt of some joke I don't understand?"

"Pinky swear."

She reached across the table. Solano locked his little finger with hers.

"Okay, then, Mr. High Roller — Mickey — what about this evening?"

She giggled like a schoolgirl.

"What are the probabilities?"

▼

The gray light of an early dawn was creeping in around the curtains of Solano's lakeside bedroom. He felt the bedclothes shift and opened his eyes to the sight of Gigi Newhouse, wonderfully naked, rising from beside him. She danced around on one foot and then the other to slip into her panties. Solano reached over his side of the bed, found her bra, and handed it to her.

"Morning," he said, ogling her appreciatively.

She strapped on her bra and sat back down to make it easy for him to fasten the hooks in place, which he did.

Then she stood up, pushed into her blouse and Daisy Dukes.

"I gotta get down the hill and go to work," she said.

She leaned down over him for a morning kiss.

"You better call me."

"You know I will," he affirmed. "You can bet on it."

She tenderly patted his crotch, shouldered her purse, and headed for the door.

"Get me some sources, will ya? I'm out on a limb with this election fraud business."

13

THE NIGHTLY news.

Maggie Morrison and Diego Ramirez traded coverage of the day's doings on KNVR's evening newscast — a tour bus crash, a house fire, a convenience store robbery, and a sympathetic public service piece on activists demonstrating at city hall for a bike path along the Truckee River.

"Now," said Ramirez, "here's our roving reporter with the latest on the Nevada senate race. It's heating up, I hear. Right, Gigi?"

The camera swiveled around to Newhouse, very soignée in a crisp blue dress, posing demurely in front of a faux work desk piled high with papers and books. A prop computer displayed glowing lists of numbers on an imitation spreadsheet. She was standing in a set that advertised investigative research.

"That's right, Diego. We've had name calling, negative ads, a scandal, and now, a disturbing development that, if confirmed, threatens the democratic process at its very core."

She turned the laptop toward the camera and pressed a key. Video of an older model Nissan Altima replaced the spreadsheet numbers. The newsroom camera zoomed in on the image.

"A few weeks ago we brought you news of Frank Osgood, who was found dead in his car. His suicide note turned out to be fake, and a murder investigation is ongoing. Now we have an explosion and fire in a house on Lake Tahoe's Nevada shore. The occupant, William Gaffney, apparently died in the blast, his body burned beyond recognition."

Newhouse's B-roll footage of the fire scene played onscreen.

"Are the deaths connected? Quite possibly so. Osgood and Gaffney were both employed by Patriotic Decision Systems, the makers of Reno's voting machines."

The TV view cut to a close-up photo of the charred label on the tablet computer case Solano recovered. In spite of the gaps, it was obvious that the singed letters spelled the Patriotic company name.

"These two men knew each other. They worked together. They were computer programmers, writing software that controls how our voting machines work.

"Recently, accusations of wrongdoing have been made by unnamed sources. Accusations of a plot to sabotage those machines, to perpetrate voter fraud in our upcoming election. Were Osgood and Gaffney involved in such a plot? Were they whistle blowers? Were they killed as part of a cover-up?"

The meager supporting evidence vanished, and the camera focused on the pretty young reporter.

"Stay tuned while we dig into this story, to confirm or refute the very serious accusations you heard here tonight. Meanwhile, if anyone out there has new information, please call our hotline. It's open twenty-four seven."

Newhouse closed the prop computer lid with a decisive snap to punctuate the end of her segment.

"Maggie? Back to you."

▼

Solano watched the show from his town house in the hills above Reno, overlooking the city.

"Attagirl, babe!"

He was gratified to see Newhouse taking action, but his upbeat mood lasted only a few minutes. Then it was back to work, looking for sucker bets in order to lose another large sum of offshore money to the Silverlode.

14

NEXT MORNING, at a socially calibrated hour, Solano placed a call to Newhouse at her mobile number. She did not pick up, and the call went to voicemail.

"Hey, you, it's Mickey. Congratulations! Your show last night, what do you call what you did? An article, story, piece, segment . . . what? Investigative reporting by any other name, though, right? Look, you're probably still asleep, I'll try you again later. Anyway, great stuff. You were great. And great looking, I might add — *am adding!*"

▼

Later on, down in town, Solano parked his Range Rover in the Safeway parking lot and spent some time examining cheap mobile telephones. The store had a dozen different models on display running on three different pay-as-you-go networks, and it took a while for Solano to piece together a strategy for anonymous communication.

After much waffling, he settled on a throwaway LG feature phone and a plastic card worth one-hundred and twenty minutes of talk time.

Back in his car he scratched a thin layer of metal off the card to reveal a long access number, which he then texted to the network to get the damn thing activated. Once that was accomplished he tentatively pressed buttons on the glass keyboard to make a confidential call.

"Good morning. Hayes and Bishop, LLP. How may I direct your call?"

"Madge? Mickey here. Is Cam around?"

"He's busy. Court filing this afternoon. But for you, sweetie — one moment, please."

On hold, instrumental versions of country western tunes flooded Solano's ear. He started his car and turned the air conditioner on high.

"Mickey! How's my boy?"

"Hey, Cam. We're good, right? Lawyer-client privilege still in force?"

"Always, slugger. Why the cloak-and-dagger?"

"I'm taking no chances."

"Okay, you're worried. What's the problem?"

"I'm trying to wiggle out of one."

"Oh? Now he tells me." The lawyer's voice did not indicate the slightest surprise.

"Yeah, it's the Silverlode. They're leaning on me to clean up a lot of offshore cash."

"The million bucks we discussed, right?"

"That and a lot more. I need to get out from under. I need advice. Your advice."

There was a noticeable pause before Hayes replied. Then, "Call the cops, why don't you?"

"Be serious. They'll nail my ass along with everyone else."

"Then just say no. Tell that guy who runs the place — Ed Barber, right? — you're done."

"I tried that. They're threatening to send the IRS a 1099 form way overstating my actual income. And worse, maybe list my ass. I'll get thrown out of every casino in the State of Nevada. There goes my life."

"You've actually been moving money for them?"

"By deliberately losing bets."

Another pause.

"Well, kiddo," said Hayes in measured tones, "looks like you're a crook. If it comes to indictment and trial, I'll defend you, of course . . . and take a chunk of your not-so-hard-earned wealth in the process. My court fee is not covered by our present arrangement."

"Ouch."

"You better hope the Feds get something else on them. Something that doesn't involve you. Regime change — that's what you need."

"How in hell is that supposed to happen?"

"Say your prayers, Mick."

▼

Solano pocketed the phone and drove to the Silverlode. There he wrote up a series of very big and very stupid bets, filling the Silverlode's sports book manager with friendly dismay.

"Mickey, Mickey, Mickey — have you gone completely crazy? You're gonna give me a heart attack."

"The Patriots pre-season? What's not to like?"

"Go on, they won't even dress Brady. That new kid? Forget about him. And damn — baseball? — the Rays? They can't hit, they can't field, they haven't won a game in more than a week."

"I like their chances, Sparkles. Big comeback."

The manager shook his head and gloomily recorded the bets.

Solano waved and strode off through the casino. He stared at the slot machines briefly, but the patterns didn't look promising, and he decided not to play.

On his way out he crossed paths with a cocktail waitress in a bikini. She was coolly patrolling the card tables, serving drinks.

"Jenny Penny," he said.

Penrose turned toward him. An initial frown gave way to a forced smile. "Mickey. How are you?"

"Downdraft. But I'll climb out."

"Sure, Mick. You always do. What I hear is, we're on the same side now." She smiled again. This time it was genuine. "That's what Dick told me. Don't let those bad bets get you down."

"I'll live." He regarded her with concealed distaste. "How about you? Down on the floor, showing some skin today."

"We're short, so I volunteered. What do you think? Do I get by in this rag?"

Penrose was nearing forty, she was in great shape, and yet she could not hope to retain her professional good looks for too many more years. Solano felt some sympathy in spite of himself.

"You look terrific," he said and meant it. But even as he spoke, his compliment caused a thought to bloom. A curious thought. A thought, he realized with a little shudder, that had been slow to arrive. "You know, I saw you on TV. You looked terrific there too. Who'd-a thunk it? Standing right beside Senator Ives, a guy with a lot of hands, according to the news report I watched."

"Oh that," she said.

Solano's sixth sense kicked in.

"You weren't really hired by the guy, were you?"

"So I'm taking one for the team. Our team. The money's good." She winked and strolled away.

▼

Outside, standing under the Reno Arch, Solano called Newhouse again. This time she picked up.

"Hi, guy. Thanks for the nice thoughts, I need 'em."

She sounded grumpy.

"You okay? What's wrong?"

"For starters? That stupid tour bus crash cost me the lead segment."

"Okay, but it's still a good story, an important story, and you broke it open."

"Says you. My editor thinks I stepped way out of line. I was hoping for some tips to come in, but the hotline is stone cold."

"It'll happen. This is big."

"So, I'm investigating residential package thefts now," she griped. "We're setting up a sting with fake boxes from Amazon. Woo-hoo."

Solano could hear her pout over the phone. "Let's get together, I'll cheer you up over dinner."

"Can't do it," said Newhouse. "I'm on tonight. Gotta stop those evil package thieves before they destroy civilization."

"I'm sure you will."

"Rain check. Say we try for next week."

"Right." Solano winced. A little rebuff there in the reporter's tone, he noticed.

"Gotta go, talk soon."

"Whoa, hang on, girl."

At the risk of further alienating his new friend, he decided to relay his latest suspicions. "Not too long ago everyone was running that story on Senator Ives' so-called *paid escort.*"

"Jennifer Penrose," said Newhouse. "I'm the one who reported her revelations of sexual assault on camera. And the guy is a married man."

"I remember. Except, Gigi, there was no sexual assault. And Ives never hired her in the first place."

"What?"

"She was hired for big bucks — by someone, don't know who — to stage the escort thing and make those charges."

"To hurt Ives' chances."

"What else?"

"Is this another one of your election fantasies? Where do you get this stuff?"

"Jenny Penny — that's what we call her — works at the Silverlode. I do a lot of business there. She told me."

"She *told* you?" Newhouse's voice was full of scorn.

"That's right. Told me, with a wink and a nod."

"Jesus, Mickey. Get a grip."

"You should check this out. I'm betting the same people who hired Ms. Penrose also wanted Osgood and Gaffney out of the way. Who are the bad guys? Russians? Right-wing crackpots? If they reached out to the Silverlode they don't have any muscle of their own. Just money to burn. Believe me, the Silverlode is not so handicapped."

There was a long silence on the other end of the line.

"Gigi?"

"I'm filing this away for future reference. If and when the smoke you're blowing ever turns into a fire."

▼

Back inside the Silverlode, Dick Worden ran into Ed Barber in the lounge behind the blackjack tables. The CEO was nursing a scotch, his first of the day.

"How's the wash?" queried Worden.

Barber put down his drink.

"We're doing okay. Repatriated about a mil-five so far."

Worden ordered coffee from a comely young waitress. As she strutted away to fetch it, he wondered briefly about Barber's private life.

"Listen, Ed. This thing is making me nervous. Our courier is a wiseass. He's made a lot of money in the biz — he's no joke, I give him that — so it's tough to dangle carrots."

Barber cocked his head, alert to the complaints and suggestions he knew were coming.

"Dick, for Christ's sake, we've been all over this. I also showed him a stick, remember?"

"Remind me."

"Drop a juicy 1099 for the IRS to feed on, list him. What more do you want?"

Worden was not convinced. "See, the problem is, the guy's too good. He's an arrogant prick, and he might think he can outsmart us."

"How's that?"

"Give us to the feds?"

Barber smiled. He was well into a long and successful career, built in part by learning how to judge character accurately. He did not doubt his assessment of the Silverlode's cooperative young gambler.

"What do you propose? Brass knuckles?"

Worden airily waved an arm. "How about we take out an ordinary bank loan for the new hotel wing?"

"Go legit?" Barber shook his head. "Too much debt. We're staggering under the load we've got, and now lenders want a piece of us. Can't let them have it."

Worden cupped a hand and drove a fist into it. "Okay then, something a little more decisive."

"Talk about causing problems," sighed Barber. "I'll think about it. Meanwhile, keep your ears open and an eye peeled. The kid may need some encouragement as we go along, but he'll play ball. He has to."

15

THE NEVADA State Senate Committee on Legislative Operations and Elections convened in Carson City to discuss the integrity of Patriotic Decision Systems' voting machines.

A dozen senators were seated in leather chairs within one of the Capitol's sumptuously wood-paneled hearing rooms, with notes before them and legislative assistants at their elbows. They were responding to accusations heard on KNVR, and picked up by various other newsgathering outfits, casting doubt on Nevada's sate-of-the-art voting technology.

Paul Toravian, Patriotic's founder and CEO, was at the brightly lit witness stand to defend his company and its products.

The committee chair studied her hand-written scribbles. "You have heard the recent accusations made in Reno, is that right, sir?"

"I'm painfully aware of the unwarranted attack on the reputation of my company's products, Madam Chairperson."

"I understand your frustration. When I try to use a computer, I'm frustrated too. Please tell me how we, public servants without technical expertise, can be expected to rely on your machines — I believe we're talking about the Ridge E-29 model — given the recent alarming accusations."

"As you no doubt know, Nevada was the first state in the country to require a paper trail to supplement the electronic tally our machines provide. The units that will be in use come November are, as you mentioned, the Ridge E-29 model, the very latest development in digital voting equipment. May I point out that these machines operate together with VeriVote — a printing system that records each and every vote on paper. The citizens of Nevada have nothing to fear — their votes will be counted, and the results will be safe and accurate and well-documented."

The chair nodded.

"Thank you for confirming your absolute confidence in the devices your company makes. But I am not as sure of the system as you are. My friends on the Gaming Control Board require each and every piece of code in a new slot machine to be verified by their own experts. Why not hand us the code you are using, so we can make a similar evaluation, boost our confidence to match your own?"

Toravian squirmed in his seat. "Our code is proprietary, Madam Chairperson. Like other trade secrets, it is protected by usage and law established over many years. With all respect, we want to assure you and the voters of Nevada that their votes will count. But we cannot be expected to do anything that might encourage a business competitor."

The committee chair smiled a condescending smile. She was not annoyed by Toravian's answer. It was exactly what she anticipated. She just wanted Patriotic's evasive legal position spelled out in the session transcript.

Toravian's political antennae told him he had not made a convincing presentation. The senator's last question, forcing him to trot out the *proprietary* argument, neatly undercut his position. Damn, that stonewall tactic never cut grease with the government. He leaned forward to continue his defense.

"If it please the committee, I will make an announcement."

"Go ahead."

"As I have said, our machines are already accurate and safe. But we have recently completed a software upgrade to make them absolutely bulletproof — our VoteRight OS version 195-dot-4-dot-1. We will be rolling out this upgrade in the coming weeks. By November, every machine in Nevada will run it."

16

THE SILVERLODE.

Offshore money.

Voting machines.

Dead programmers.

Election fraud.

Jennifer Penrose.

Solano was pacing the floor of his Lake Tahoe home office in mental turmoil. Was there a connection between his employers and election fraud? Good question. His sixth sense wasn't always reliable, but he pinned the probability near certainty.

"Hah!" He clapped his hands. "I think my casino pals might have made a mistake. A little one, anyway. And maybe . . . maybe a big one."

Jenny Penny, the Silverlode security babe, formerly icy and now friendly, she was the mistake.

What had him on his feet, anxiously walking back and forth, unable to concentrate, was a more serious question: how to use said connection to work out from under Ed Barber's thumb and free himself from the prospect of criminal prosecution.

"There must be a way," he muttered. "But I'm damned if I see it."

He strolled out onto his dock with a cold beer. A summer wind was stirring up white caps a hundred yards out from shore.

Three slugs and his beer was drained.

In addition to his WaveRunner, he also owned a Reinell 185 motorboat capable of pulling a skier, and a second-hand Fanatic sailboard. He considered a jaunt on the board, but decided against it.

Back in the kitchen, he tossed the empty bottle under his brushed-metal sink, reached into his brushed-metal refrigerator for another beer, and downed it without enjoyment.

He carried a third beer to his desk where, to distract himself, he started his computer and cracked open his email reader. He rarely looked at his messages, and they were queued up hundreds deep. He scrolled down through the spam and the scams and paused over a cryptic note from July:

> *look & u will find it*

The note was tagged 'sent from mobile,' but there was no signature. What the hell? Unsolicited religious crap? A lame phishing attempt? He moved the message into his junk mail folder and there, with all possible malicious internet links disabled, he examined the details. Contrary to expectations, it looked legit, like a real message from a real person. Someone wanted him to find something. Find what?

He almost never entertained. A cleaning lady kept the place in order on a bi-weekly basis. Other than that, Gaffney had paid a visit just before his house burned down, and then Gigi spent the night . . .

Hmm.

On the message header he noted an AOL address. Good Christ, the email service cavemen once used. He then scoured his contact list for a match. It took a while before he found it. Long ago, when he and Bill Gaffney were both at HighScore, an AOL address was his colleague's way of dodging corporate scrutiny while offering scurrilous gossip and politically incorrect observations about women in the workforce.

Solano felt the hair on his arms rising. Gaffney! That screwball! He planted something. What did he plant?

Curiosity aroused, he methodically searched the house, opened all the cabinets and drawers, checked his mailbox, even looked into the storage container on his dock. *Nada.* Whatever *it* was, if present somewhere on his property, *it* was well hidden.

The effort and the beer combined to give Solano a throbbing headache. He gave up the search and pivoted into the downstairs bathroom. There he washed his hands and ran cold water over his face.

After toweling off, he opened the medicine chest and reached for his ibuprofen supply. He tipped the bottle to shake out a couple of tablets.

Whoops — along with the medicine out fell a thin plastic rectangle, the size of a fingernail.

"Well, hello there."

He held it up between thumb and forefinger. He was looking at a SanDisk thirty-two gigabyte *MicroSD memory card.*

▼

Solano inserted the card into a standard SD adapter and inserted the combination into the SD card reader on his laptop computer.

A window opened with a single folder on display:

```
DOT-RED
```

An odd name. He clicked on the folder. It opened in turn. Now he was staring at a half dozen files:

```
assignedvars.red
declarations.red
inlinecorral.red
legacyblock.red
manageupdate.red
newfunctionbin.red
```

Strange, he thought. He clicked on *newfunctionbin.red* and directed his computer to open it with his text editor. What he saw puzzled him:

```
nav>>>pds195>>>f*sb*pro{{ief=tr3+vtp[3];mv=cr+ip
+*id*;flsh;}};:cx:f*gtk*pro{{scm=f*pll*tls;}};:r
t:f*hor*pro{{qrp=f*pll*gvt;srt{i=enm;i<=0;i++;}}
e=zxq<r>pto<r>enm;}}} . . .
```

There was a lot more. The text went on endlessly for pages and pages. It was obviously computer code, but jammed together in unreadable form by the author and possibly given some form of primitive encryption. Solano was a former code stallion and self-confessed geekster, but he had never seen anything like it. No recognizable commands were visible. No mathematical or logical statements revealed any purpose. Not only was the code impenetrable, but apart from all the curly braces and semicolons, features of the *C* family of computer languages, he didn't even know what kind of programming was involved. He was lost.

He surmised that Gaffney, when he quit, had walked out of Patriotic Decision Systems with the code in his pocket.

"And, you bastard — you dropped this damn banana peel for me to slip on."

17

A SUMMER EVENING in Reno.

Wilbur Rollins Guyette was hanging around the entrance to Fulton Alley on Sierra Street near West 3rd.

The narrow lane, a block and a half from the Reno Arch, was flanked by tall buildings, and even in the lingering summer twilight it was cloaked in shadow. He was moving back and forth, now into the bright lights of the broad avenue, now into the gloom of the alley itself, where his dark gray coveralls rendered him nearly invisible. His eyes were staring. His fingers were twitching. He was on the prowl for any opportunity.

A block away, Mickey Solano and Gigi Newhouse exited Bangkok, a very nice Thai restaurant, where they had just finished a meal following the early KNVR newscast. Solano was hoping to see her again later on, but she declined, pleading exhaustion after a performance on camera. They kissed and parted.

Solano watched her walk away in her spiffy on-the-air clothes. He was confused. Her mood at dinner had been cool, and his hopeful invitation was refused. Something to think about. He turned around and hiked over to West Street where his Range Rover was waiting.

Newhouse was heading toward her own car and the TV station, where she was prepared to reveal the perpetrators of Reno's recent wave of package thefts on the late show. She was lugging the uneaten portion of her Pad Kee Mao in a styrofoam box. She was humming to herself.

At the entrance to Fulton Alley, Guyette sprang out of hiding to confront her.

"Whoa there, lady, I'll take that purse."

Newhouse inhaled sharply and backpedaled. She jammed her hand into her purse and scratched around for the canister of pepper spray she always carried.

Guyette took a menacing step toward her.

She whipped out the pepper spray and took aim.

"Get away from me, you creep!"

Guyette paused. "Hey, I know you! You're that TV reporter. All that crime shit, election shit. Well, well, how about that?"

Newhouse looked all around, desperately hoping for a cop, or a passerby, or any kind of assistance, but the street was empty.

Guyette took another step. Before Newhouse could activate her spray, Guyette swatted the canister out of her hand.

"Ahhh!" she cried.

He tugged at her purse.

"Gimme!"

She resisted.

"Oh yeah?"

Wham!

He drew back and slammed a fist into her face. Down she went on her butt. Her Pad Kee Mao and her purse went flying.

Guyette collected the purse and ran off down the alley, throwing car fob, cell phone, lipstick, facial tissues, tampons, vitamin pills, everything except her wallet onto the pavement as he disappeared into the shadows.

Newhouse remained sprawled on her back. She felt her face where a big bruise was rising. She tasted blood and delicately ran her tongue around her mouth, terrified that a tooth might have been broken. Her cheek was spongy, but her smile would return . . . someday.

"Ohhh . . . fuck . . ."

Hot tears welled up. She dissolved into racking sobs.

SEPTEMBER

18

NEWS of the day.

On TV the KNVR logo came and went. The house fires, wildfires, and car crashes came and went. A soldier returning home from Afghanistan came and went. Labor Day festivities came and went.

After a pause for commercials, Maggie Morrison, who was leading the charge on the late night broadcast, then turned her attention to the political topic of the moment.

"It's labor day. And no one needs a break more than our candidates for US senate. The race is heating up, and they're both working hard to gain voter trust and approval. Here's Senator Ives with his pitch to Nevada . . ."

Ives appeared on camera at the groundbreaking ceremony for a new Procter & Gamble distribution center on Reno's outskirts.

"My friends, I'm standing in front of a bare patch of Mother Earth. Soon, a building, a very big building, will rise behind me. Nevada has relied on gambling and America's many sins too long. I'm a gambler myself. I'm gambling you will vote for me later in the fall" — cheers and chuckles from a small crowd — "but we need to move on, work ourselves into the mainstream economy of America. My cynical opponent thinks he can fool you with empty promises. My plan will provide the funds to develop Nevada's infrastructure, to make it easier for companies to come here with their good will and good jobs."

The cheers and shouts of encouragement were cut off as the newscast refocused on Morrison.

"Now here's Paxton," she said. "The challenger is a newcomer, but polls show him closing the gap . . ."

The scene shifted to Paxton, speaking to a Rotary Club audience in Las Vegas.

"What I'm going to do when I'm elected is change the business climate of our state. We can no longer rely on the feeble efforts of my scandal-ridden opponent. The time for old-time government hand-holding is over. And the same thing goes for the old-timer I'm running against. We are going to deregulate, let your business minds innovate, let you invest your money where it will pay off in prosperity, and not drop into bureaucracy's bottomless tax pit. Are you with me?"

Loud shouts and clapping were dialed down as Morrison reappeared in the studio.

"Well, there you have it. Candidates at each other's throats. Whatever happened to courtesy and compromise? Politics gets uglier every day — and it may be trending to violence. Here's Diego with the latest . . ."

The camera dollied over to Ramirez, standing in the middle of the set that usually framed Newhouse.

"It's a sad night here at KNVR. Two days ago our political reporter Gigi Newhouse was accosted and beaten right here on the streets of our city. Although she will recover, her wounds will take some time to heal. Was it a mugging? Was it sexual assault? Or . . . was it political? Ms. Newhouse has reported from the emergency room that the attacker cited her commitment to political stories even as the blows fell."

Ramirez gestured toward the prop laptop on the set's fake desk. An archive photo on the little screen showed Newhouse smiling radiantly. He gently closed the computer lid.

"Good night, Gigi, get well soon."

19

SOLANO WAS IN his Reno town house surrounded by TV screens. The news was running, but he missed the item on Gigi Newhouse, because the audio was muted, and because he was obsessively examining computer code. Obscure computer code. Code that he was determined to crack.

He was undaunted by the hopelessly opaque text and searched methodically through each of the files he had located on Gaffney's MicroSD card. His persistence paid off with a small discovery. The code wasn't actually encrypted, just very terse. Impossible to understand, but well-formed, like this:

```
f*cvr*prt*(t:ctz,ta:enm){rt cvr$ctz<r>enm;}
```

He studied the snippet he had extracted from the reams of apparent nonsense. The *f* might stand for *function,* possibly named *cvr.* He thought **prt** might mean *prototype.* The parenthesis looked like it held parameters. That is, if the **colons** signaled *type declarations.* The statement inside the curly braces was strange, but **enm** might stand for *enum,* and the function's purpose might be to extract some value from an enumerated list. Or not.

"Shit," he said. "How can anyone write gibberish like this?"

Solano leaned back and cast an eye on his other screens. The KNVR weatherman was finishing up his sign-off summary. Going to be hot tomorrow. The newscast was over. He dialed Newhouse's number, just in case she might want to share a nightcap.

The call went to voicemail.

"You've almost reached Gigi Newhouse. I can't promise to return your call, but I do promise to listen to your message, after the beep."

Solano almost hung up without a word, but changed his mind.

"Hey, Gigi, it's Mickey, checking in. I'm onto something. When it cracks, you get the story. Call me if you want some company . . . or if not, well, that's okay too . . . anyway, sweet dreams."

He cradled his phone, opened a web browser, and submitted his more-or-less coherent code sample to the electronic tentacles of Google for identification. He wasn't expecting anything, but both the Stack Overflow and Wikipedia websites listed some possibilities:

> *Atomix*
> *Bolo*
> *Omnium*
> *Quantor*
> *Redstone*
> *S4*
> *Sapphire*
> *Yolo*

Somewhere in the past, he had heard the name *Bolo,* but he knew nothing about it. Was *Yolo* a *Bolo* variant? Or did the name come from a county in California? Or did it reference the jock acronym for *You Only Live Once* — what he was busy doing. Living on the edge of exhaustion at that. He chuckled inwardly at the conceptual gap between his inquiring mind and his tired and ignorant guesses.

The other languages cited were a complete mystery. Except, hmm, the files on his computer were all appended with the *dot-red* suffix. *Redstone?* Maybe so.

While he was searching online for a decent description of Redstone's syntax and usage, his eyes closed involuntarily. He put his head down on folded arms and fell asleep at his desk.

20

SOLANO WOKE UP to a telephone call from his accountant, Jacob Quarles.

"Jake, my man. It's early."

"Just wanted to let you know, as we discussed, that another two-hundred-K has appeared in the Sporting Insights account."

"Shit. Uhh, which bet?"

"From the Silverlode, but the money was a wire-transfer, so who knows? Another big win — you remember, right? I mean, you're moving fortunes back and forth."

"I'm foggy. Sorry."

"And this on top of the two-hundred-K that already appeared. I called you and left a message. You listened, I hope."

"Crap, another big win. Remind me, when did you first see it?"

Quarles was silent for a moment. Then, "Couple of weeks, looks like. Gotta say, you are the man. Well, you are when you win. When you win."

"Right. I'm a winner. Time to re-invest that loot."

"Wisely, my friend. Look — you're down as far as up these days. Instead of gambling it all away, why not buy some real estate?"

"I've already got two houses, Jake."

"Okay, pick up a share in one of the office buildings here in town. Or even Vegas. I know some developers, they could use —"

"Nope, nope, nope. The cobbler's gotta stick to his . . . whatever the hell it's called."

"Last," said Quarles.

"Last. Gotta stick to my last."

▼

Solano looked for some losing propositions among the day's later games, but his sixth sense didn't flag any contests likely to go one way or the other. In any case, his mind was occupied with computer code, not sports book spreads.

On the way into town he bypassed the Silverlode and parked outside Balzac's Books.

There, in the technical section, he plowed through every programming book he could find, soaking up information on the Redstone computer language.

The umpteenth O'Reilly tome provided some insight:

> Redstone uses C-family syntax and conventional imperative structure in a functional paradigm. It is, in effect, a pseudo-functional language. Like Haskell, it embodies the lambda calculus, with fixed inputs and lazy evaluation. It excels in parallel processing and freely allows expansion of its domain without internal rewriting.

In another book, *Red Meat for Dummies,* he learned a little more:

> Redstone was crafted by DARPA as an easy and graceful alternative to Haskell. Among its many virtues is an inbuilt obfuscation capability that is robust. Its main application, until recently, has been in embedded systems, particularly cruise missiles and UAVs, where the possibility of casualties — interception or crash in hostile territory — might expose code to enemy eyes.

Yet a third book, *Embedded Essentials,* explained why a company like Patriotic Decision Systems might favor Redstone's use:

> Commercial developers are turning to Redstone and its even more stringent variant, Atomic Redstone, to write software for civilian embedded systems where the language syntax emphasizes safety, where static analysis can ferret out all bugs, and where obfuscation conceals functionality from competitors.

Further inquiry informed Solano that the obfuscation executable would be found in a source file called *obtuse.red.*

"Damn," he said aloud. "I don't have that file."

▼

He was far from his goal of decoding the little MicroSD card Gaffney left him, but he was starting to make some progress, and he was excited.

He jumped back in his Range Rover and called Newhouse to share the latest developments. The call went to voicemail.

"Not again . . ." he muttered.

He revved up his SUV and headed for KNVR, bypassing the Silverlode again.

At the station, in spite of several failed calls, he approached the receptionist in a lighthearted mood.

"Gigi Newhouse, please. Is she around?"

"And your name?"

"Mickey Solano. I'm a friend," he said. The receptionist adopted a neutral expression. "A good friend," he added, with a smile and a head angled to establish the nature of the relationship.

The receptionist scowled. Solano assumed she didn't believe he actually knew the reporter. But no . . .

"Goodness, Mister — ahh — Solano. Miss Newhouse isn't here, she's on leave."

Solano was taken aback. "What? Her stories are hot, don't tell me some politico twisted your arm —"

"It's nothing like that. Didn't you see the news last night?"

"Whoops, no, working on a project. We're both kind of busy these days."

"Well, as Diego reported, Miss Newhouse was attacked and beaten on the street downtown a couple of nights ago."

Solano was stunned. "We had dinner a couple of nights ago. Downtown. Gigi had to get back to the studio."

He stiffened, trying to remember the sequence of events. Then he threw up his hands.

"What happened?" he growled.

The receptionist cringed. "I don't have any details."

Solano's mind was racing. "She's been to my house, up on the lake . . ."

"Sounds romantic," allowed the receptionist, nodding mechanically.

"But I've never been to her house. Where does she live?"

"Oh, I'm sorry, Mr. Solano, I can't give you her address." She lifted a mobile phone and pointed instructively at it. "You could leave a message."

Solano realized he was scaring the receptionist. He took a deep breath to recover his composure, waved his thanks, and seated himself in a waiting area near the desk. He entered Newhouse's number on his own phone, expecting voicemail. But Newhouse answered on the third ring.

"Gigi? Hey, babe, tell me you're okay."

"Mickey?"

"Yeah, it's me. How ya doin'?"

"The doctors say the bruises are superficial. Tell that to my pain center. But, whoopee, my winning smile will continue to light up TV screens."

"Oh, good, that's good, good to hear."

"Right. Just not for several weeks."

"Huh?"

"My face — I look like a squirrel with a mouthful of nuts." She laughed self-consciously.

"You always look good to me. What can I do? Can I come over? Bring you something? Soup? Ice cream?"

"No, no. I'm okay. Give me a week or two."

"Week or two — ?"

"Tell you what, I'll call you when I feel presentable, how's that?"

Solano wasn't letting go. "Listen, this will cheer you up — I have the sabotage code Osgood wrote. On my computer. It's hard to read, but I'm making progress."

"Mickey . . ."

"Sorry, I know you're hurting, but this is exciting."

"Enough already. The guy who hit me knew who I was." In her memory, the man's offhand remarks had grown into threats. "Was I just mugged, or was it deliberate intimidation?"

"A warning, huh? — that plays right into our theories," bubbled Solano, as if he was hearing good news.

"Your theories, Mickey. Not mine. *Sheesh."*

21

AT HOME on a beautifully sunny Lake Tahoe day, Solano chose study over recreation. He spent some time with the little MicroSD card looking for the mysterious file *obtuse.red* without success. Then his throwaway phone rang.

"Solano. How'd you get this number?"

"You gave it to me, Mickey. Remember? Stay under the radar?"

The voice on the line belonged to Ed Barber. He didn't sound happy.

"Oh, hi, Ed. How are things?"

"Could be better. What's the matter with you?"

"Nothing that I know of. Working on stuff."

"Busy boy, huh?"

"If this is about your latest deposit — my latest so-called win, I'm on it."

"You better be. You're earning interest on four-hundred-thousand dollars that belongs to the Silverlode."

"I thought I won a big bet."

"Don't get cute with me, cutie-pie. Why aren't you losing our money?"

"Um, it's baseball season. Most games, you know, they could go either way. I'm looking at the sheets, I'll be playing, don't worry."

"As excuses go, that's a good one, actually believable, I'll let it pass."

"Appreciate it," said Solano, cautiously maintaining a respectful attitude.

"Why am I even talking to you?" mused Barber rhetorically. "I guess it's 'cause I like you, got a soft spot. Otherwise, I'd get Dick Worden to knock some sense into your thick skull."

"Football starts this weekend. Different story, you'll see."

"Now listen here, kid. We have an arrangement. You help us, we hand you a nice cut. We all do well, right?"

"So it seems."

"Let me hear you say it." There was a hard edge in Barber's usually silky delivery.

Solano dropped his forehead onto his desk in shame and frustration. Then he lifted it back up. "We have an arrangement," he agreed.

"And you are going to honor it," insisted Barber.

"And I'm going to honor it. Yes I am."

"All right then. Good old Sparkles will be waiting for you."

Click.

Ominously, the line went dead.

Solano had never been called to account by the Silverlode brass before. He resented Barber's casually superior tone, the man's bald commands. Something was going on, he decided. Some change of plans, a corporate policy shift. What it might be, however, he did not know.

"Blah blah blah," he muttered. "Ed Barber, the Silverlode toad. Croak why don't you?"

▼

In the Silverlode's upstairs offices, Dick Worden and Ed Barber were having a discussion. Both sensed trouble on the horizon, and both were uncertain about the best way to contain it.

"That guy Voss, from the Control Board. He had a subpoena," noted Worden.

"He did. That he did," said Barber, sounding tired and a lot less sure of himself than Solano would have guessed.

"And we answered it with memos."

"That too."

"With the outcome in the hands of a fucking nest of legal eagles."

"Could be difficult, I know," sighed Barber.

"So Voss talks to a judge. The judge issues the paper . . . on what grounds?" Where did Mr. Voss get probable cause?"

"The burning question."

"I'll say," snorted Worden. "Our problem? We made a deal with a kid who doesn't know the rules of the road, shows no proper sense of respect . . ."

"He's got the chops, a history of big bets, looks good to the auditors."

"The auditors we pay to make *everything* look good."

"At no inconsiderable cost at that," conceded Barber.

"There's more. Jenny told me she ran into Solano here in the shop. They kissed and made up."

"Nice to have a happy family."

Worden rolled his eyes. "Not literally. They talked. He knew she wasn't actually hired by Ives."

"Why would he care? He's on our side." Barber was confused.

Worden kicked the open office door shut and took a seat in front of Barber's desk.

"I don't think so. We can't trust that slimeball, no matter how much we're paying him. I talked to his lawyer."

"You what?"

"Cameron Hayes. Hazy Cam. Everyone knows the guy, why not?"

"Go ahead."

"He plays his cards close, but he admitted that there's no love lost between his give-a-shit client and the Silverlode."

Barber leaned back, placed his hands behind his head, and stared at the ceiling. He appeared lost in thought. After a while he sat up straight, brought his hands down, and slapped the desktop.

"You think Solano ratted us out to the Control Board?"

"Yeah, Ed. I know you like the kid . . ."

"But Solano is in this up to his neck. Were he to testify, if it comes to that, he'll go down long before we do."

"You think so? Willing to take the chance? Hayes hinted at immunity if the situation slides south."

"Good God. We can't have that."

"No sirree. We should call the doctor."

"That would focus the spotlight on us."

"Nahh. Look at it this way — cops will see how our pigeon got in way over his head, how he offended some heavy dudes. Untouchable dudes, you know?"

"Imaginary wiseguys." Barber scratched his nose. "Cops do love that fairy-tale mob stuff, it explains a lot of unsolvable crimes. The doctor, huh?"

The Silverlode boss wasn't entirely sure about the idea, but his chief lieutenant was.

"Call the man. Let him prescribe a cure."

22

SOLANO WAS DISTRACTED. On one hand, he owed the Silverlode a ton of its own money. On the other, he had incriminating computer code sitting on his hard drive, an irresistible puzzle he was itching to solve. On top of everything else, he was worried about Gigi Newhouse, down for the count after a mugging. A mugging or a hit, he didn't know which.

He dialed her number. The call went to voicemail. He hung up and dialed the station. The KNVR receptionist stopped him cold with some unexpected news.

"I'm sorry she's not picking up, Mr. Solano. She's probably very busy, settling into her new job in Portland."

"Say what?" Solano was shocked.

"She's taken a position at our sister station, KGW. Editing, working in the background until her face heals up."

"When did this happen?" He could feel the blood draining out of his face.

"This week. It's very sudden. We're all as surprised as you are."

"New job — Portland — KGW."

"That's right, they had a vacancy. She went to Oregon State, did you know that? She's a great fit."

"Don't doubt it."

"You take care, Mr. Solano."

▼

Solano called KGW and found himself trapped in the tangled vines of a robotic answering service. After many futile key presses and a half-dozen desperate pleas for an agent or an operator, he finally reached a live associate. He asked for Newhouse.

"Miss Newhouse isn't available, sir."

"I'm a friend from Reno. We missed a chance to talk in all the confusion, new job, busy moving, both of us really tied up with work. I need a break on this. Please help me get in touch."

"Here's voicemail, her new account. Best I can do. Have a great Northwest K-G-W day."

Solano left a brief message and jammed the phone into a pocket. His new girlfriend was slipping away. He didn't know exactly how he felt about her, but as with all bets, he absolutely hated losing.

"No no no. You do not get off so easy, babe."

▼

Seven hours later, following a nonstop Alaska flight from Reno to Portland, he was renting a car at PDX. Soon he was rolling along leafy green Southwest Jefferson Street, checking out the KGW-TV studio.

He didn't have any information about Newhouse's new duties, her address, or her new telephone numbers, if any, but it turned out that he didn't need them. On his second pass by the station, he noticed a Silver Lexus SUV with Nevada plates exit the parking lot, right in front of his rental car. The driver was silhouetted in late afternoon light, but he could tell by her posture, her baseball cap, and the way she turned her head that it was Newhouse. He jumped on her tail and followed her through grinding rush hour traffic, east across the Willamette River on the Morrison bridge, and onward into the Laurelhurst neighborhood.

Newhouse left her car in the driveway of a small house on a narrow tree-lined street and headed for the front door toting a bag full of groceries. Solano parked at the curb, leaped from his car, and waved.

"Gigi!"

Newhouse spun around to see who was calling her name. When she recognized Solano, her swollen face turned white. She waved shyly and struggled with unfamiliar keys to unlock her door.

Solano marched across the lawn toward her, cheerfully waving a bouquet of yellow roses.

Newhouse covered her face with one hand, managed to get her door open with the other, and ducked inside. The door closed firmly behind her and locked with an audible *snick.*

Solano was unprepared for her reaction. He knocked. Newhouse did not answer.

"Gigi, what the hell? Talk to me."

He knocked again. Still no answer.

"Well, damn."

He touched the reporter's contact number on his smartphone. He heard her phone ring, amazing in itself, and was surprised when, instead of letting the call drop into voicemail, she actually picked up.

"Mickey. How did you find me? What do you want?"

Solano pulled the phone away from his ear in a gesture of astonishment. He was having a long distance conversation with someone less than ten feet away.

"Uhh, you," he said. "I want you. I hear Portland has great food. Come on out, I'll take you to dinner."

"No, Mickey. I can't."

"We don't have to talk about elections, although there's blood in the water, and I'm circling like a shark."

"Sure you are. But I'm not on anyone's menu, thanks. Been there, done that."

"Got it. Understood. Say, nice place you found."

"I'm renting for now."

Solano waved his arms to take in the urban forest canopy overhead. "Look at all this foliage. We can talk about trees."

"Forget it. Go home. Jesus, what does it take?"

"I'm not giving up on you."

"Oh yes you are. I'm not Sy Hersh. I'm a shallow ambitious kid looking for an easy break."

"You are being way too hard on yourself."

"Listen, Mickey. Don't you get it? You attract trouble like a dookie draws flies. Stay away from me."

She ended the call.

Solano stared at the door for a few seconds. Then he gently deposited his bouquet on the tiny porch and retreated to his rental car. He was sliding behind the wheel when Newhouse's door cracked open. A hand reached out and snagged the flowers.

Solano whistled grimly through clenched teeth. He was hurt by his failure to win back the reporter, but he couldn't pin down the source of his pain. Losing a lover? Or just losing a damn bet? The emotional fog told him his wounds weren't deep and, oddly, cleared his head.

He started the car and drove away.

23

SOLANO RETURNED to Reno in a somber mood.

His flight from Portland, via Seattle, touched down in the wee hours. The night air was balmy, the indigo sky was quilted with stars, and the city was suffused in its twenty-four-hour glow. But the charms of the familiar high desert territory did little to cheer him up.

He considered going to bed, but he wasn't sleepy, just morose. He made coffee in case his eyelids grew heavy and sat down at the desk in his Reno town house. There he started taking notes on terrible gambling prospects, prepping for a trip to the Silverlode later in the day.

Soon enough his curiosity about Osgood's computer files distracted him from the business at hand. He thought about one file in particular, *manageupdate.red,* speculatively envisioning a decryption tool embedded in the opaque text. If he were hiding such a tool, that's where he would have put it. He entered the search word *obtuse* into his text editor, but all he saw for his efforts was *word not found.*

"Shit."

Solano felt a sharp pang of disappointment lance through his chest. The feeling puzzled him. His offhand search gambit was a long shot, that he knew, and the negative result was just another routine setback, anticipated even. So why the sting?

Solano was unaccustomed to introspection, never spent a lot of time analyzing life choices, but suddenly all his actions seemed suspect. Thinking it over, he slowly allowed himself to realize that he didn't have a real plan to salvage his good name, just a reckless notion of performing some heroic deed to redeem his mistakes. A wave of disgust washed over him.

He shuffled into his living room and stared out east toward the Virginia Range mountains rimming the Washoe County basin. The sun was already up.

He blinked, picked up his throwaway phone, and called his lawyer.

"Cam, if I get in trouble, how would the DA prosecute me? Felony or misdemeanor? Based on what I've been doing or how much I've been doing it?"

Hayes was circumspect. "Lunch at Campania on the river. Explanations at twelve-thirty."

▼

When Solano arrived at the restaurant, a comfortably old-fashioned downtown hangout for businessmen, Hayes was already there and already into his second margarita. He beckoned his client to a table covered in a white tablecloth that was dressed up with damask napkins, shiny utensils, and little roses in a vase. They shook hands. An ancient waiter dressed in a starched white jacket appeared with bread and olive oil. Solano ordered a beer.

"So, kid, here's what I know," said Hayes, lacing his fingers together. "Should the prosecutor take an interest, he would go before a grand jury, and since you're an innocent-looking first-time offender, he would persuade them to indict based on money. The fact that you are wealthy stirs resentment among your fellow citizens, as you may have guessed."

"Yeah, I get it."

"But the real money question is how much cloth you have laundered. That's what makes the case important. That million bucks you told me about . . . not good, laddie."

Solano groaned. "And another six hundred thousand or so since then."

"Lot of dough."

"Tell me."

The waiter returned. They both ordered elegant little pizzettas.

"But that's not your problem, unless the investigators can unravel the Silverlode's accounting practices. The casino is good, their books are probably well disguised, so maybe not."

"I like that idea."

"No you don't. I had a conversation with a guy. The Silverlode is worried about you, about your loyalty."

"Who? Who did you talk to? Barber? That jerk Worden?"

Their food arrived. Between bites, Hayes laid out his concerns. "Doesn't matter. What's important is their attitude. They don't think you love them."

"Hah. I don't."

"And that's your problem. The cops? Fuck 'em. But the Silverlode has the ways and means to make your life unpleasant. Or worse, short."

"What are we talking about? The mob?"

Hayes snorted contemptuously. "They're not the mob. And neither am I, in case you're wondering. But they know people, silent partners some of them, and they have old-fashioned ideas."

He paused to let the information sink in.

"You want peace and tranquility, Mick? Be a good boy. No lip. Bow and scrape and get the Silverlode money back into their accounts as fast as possible."

"I'm trying."

"Try harder."

Hayes went to work on his pizzetta. Solano's attention floated around the room. A dozen other tables were busy with chattering diners telling jokes, making deals; all of them apparently happy, prosperous, and smugly secure in the bosom of democratic America.

"You watching the senate race, Cam?"

"What's that got to do with anything?"

"Election fraud. Someone is tinkering with our voting machines."

"Impossible. Are you nuts?" Hayes squinted at his client. His expression suggested doubts about the gambler's mental health.

"That scandal in the news," continued Solano defensively, "Ives and the girl? The girl is Jenny Penny, Silverlode skin. She was paid by the opposition. A setup."

"Holy guacamole, kiddo, you worry me."

"If I can connect the dots, I'm free."

"You aren't in trouble enough? You want to be a *dot* now?"

"I know what I'm doing," insisted Solano.

Hayes finished his margarita. He dropped a fifty and a twenty on the table and stood up. He checked his watch. "Preliminary hearing. Gotta scramble. Lunch is on me."

"Thanks, Cam."

"But if we wind up in court, if you live that long, that's on you."

"Right." Solano nodded. He felt small, and to assert his battered ego, he offered a tip. "You want some action? Try Mariners over the A's tonight. The Maniac is pitching for Oakland. He doesn't have it."

"Your sixth sense at work?"

"Definitely. I'm betting the other way."

"Good for you."

Hayes patted Solano on the shoulder and strolled away.

▼

At the Silverlode, Solano wound his way through the ranks of slot machines, past the blackjack dealers, past the craps and roulette tables, and into the sports book. There he signaled Eric Sparling and placed half a dozen big bets that were almost guaranteed to lose.

"Mickey, what's wrong with you? I don't get it," said Sparling, in the gentle tones used by bartenders on hopeless bar flies.

Solano almost confessed his purpose, but stopped short when he realized that the book manager's concerns were genuine.

"Not your problem, Sparkles."

Sparling nodded sagely, becoming vaguely aware that something he didn't understand was going on. "You're right," he said, with a deep frown, "It's not. You'll be off the schneid and back on top in no time, Mick."

Solano gave him a little salute.

"You know I will."

24

TWO DAYS LATER, restored by sleep and the perversely satisfying loss of all his recent bets, Solano was in his Reno home, staring at TV screens. He was simultaneously absorbing sports info and working on the Patriotic voting code, undaunted by his lawyer's warnings.

The door bell rang.

Solano switched the TV feed from *SportsCenter* to a closed-circuit surveillance camera. It revealed a young man in a polo shirt and slacks standing at his front door. A cop in casual dress, the same one who previously showed up at his house on the lake. What was that guy's name?

Solano leaned toward the monitor. "Who is it, please?"

His voice blared through a speaker over the front door, startling the policeman.

"Officer Voss, Mr. Solano."

"Trixie, unlock the front door," ordered Solano.

"Unlocking Grand Hall Entryway. Your primary residence is now insecure," warned the audiobot.

"So I'm taking a chance, stop nagging."

Solano padded into the foyer and opened the door partway. "I remember you now. Luke Voss, right? What's up?"

"I need you to ride downtown with me. Official interview," said Voss.

"That doesn't sound like fun. Why would I do that?"

"Because, if you come along voluntarily, I won't have to perform an actual arrest."

Solano scowled. "Interview? In a little room somewhere with no windows? I want my lawyer."

"You won't need him. It's not really about you. Let's just talk."

"Like on those TV cop shows where the bad guy always confesses? No thanks."

Voss chuckled. "You know your TV. Go ahead, call your lawyer, we'll have a party."

Solano reached for a landline handset and dialed Cameron Hayes' office. The attorney sighed and agreed to meet at the Reno Police Department on East 2nd Street.

▼

Voss was driving a Dodge Charger. The glass was missing from the passenger side window, and a sheet of translucent plastic had been duct-taped to the frame in its place.

Voss donned a pair of Ray-Ban sunglasses. Solano demonstrated his refusal to be intimidated by slipping on a pair of fancy Oakleys.

The plastic window covering rippled and chattered in the wind as the car rolled down the hill. While he drove, Voss made a proposal.

"See, what we want to do, Mr. Solano —"

"Mickey."

"— okay, Mickey — we want you to be seen handing money to the Silverlode brass, either Ed Barber or Dick Worden. We'll put you on video."

The idea was so preposterous that Solano actually laughed aloud. "How dumb am I? That would be the end of my gambling career."

Voss stared coldly at Solano through his sunglasses. "It's already the end, pal. You need to cooperate."

Solano returned the stare through his own sunglasses. "I'm a clean machine, your threats mean nothing."

"Oh really? Bet? I like the odds."

Solano shook his head. Voss was a cop, but he sounded like a naïve teenager. "Don't bet against me, officer. I'm a pro. You will lose."

▼

Voss turned onto McCarran Boulevard. As they descended the long slope into the Reno basin a green Vespa emerged from one of the housing developments and trailed along behind them. The rider was wearing black coveralls and gloves. His face was concealed behind a dark visor on a silver helmet.

▼

Voss parked on 2nd street beside a seedy motel near the police station. He stepped out and gestured toward the building.

"Not really my gig, but it's a convenient spot for a serious conversation."

"You mean, *taped* conversation. I don't see my lawyer," groused Solano.

"Right. It's hot, let's wait inside."

Voss led the way along the sidewalk. They were about to jaywalk across the street to the police building when the green Vespa that had been on their tail zipped past, cutting them off.

"Hey, watch yourself!" shouted Voss.

The Vespa squealed to a halt. The rider turned in his saddle. There was a handgun with a long barrel in his hand. He leveled the weapon.

Pow!

Voss staggered backward and went down at the curb. The Vespa sped away down the street.

"Oh shit! Oh no!" yelped Solano.

Voss was on his back on the sidewalk, unconscious, but breathing. A large red patch under his right breast was staining his polo shirt.

"Oh Jesus," mumbled Solano. "Oh! Oh! Oh!" He dropped to his knees and pressed his hands over the wound.

"Whoa, Voss, hang on, gonna be fine, gonna be okay, be okay!"

He raised his head and scanned the area.

"Help, somebody! Got a man shot here! Little help!"

Voss' breathing was becoming labored. Solano could hear bubbly sounds each time he exhaled. Punctured lung? Oh my God.

"Help! Hey, help!"

After what seemed like an hour, a passerby approached. When the person, a woman who might have been a hooker, saw the situation, she started to cross the street. Solano waved strenuously with a bloody hand. She reluctantly altered course.

"What happened, Jack?" she said.

"My, uhh, friend here, he just got shot. I need —"

"Oh no you don't." She saw blood and raised her hands to push the sight away. "Not my scene. Whoo, I'ma go bye-bye."

She turned away, but Solano grabbed an ankle before she could take a step. He fumbled in a pocket for his telephone. After an eternal struggle he managed to free it from his pants. He tossed it to the woman.

"For the love of God, lady, dial 9-1-1!"

25

THE VESPA RIDER was sitting on a picnic table in suburban Manzanita Park, not far from the towering Atlantis Casino Resort, and miles away from the scene of his crime. His helmet was on the table beside him. His little scooter was parked nearby.

Unmasked, he was a small fellow with sharp features and sandy hair. He spent some time talking on a little flip phone. When the call ended, he removed the device's SIM card and cut it into tiny pieces with a nail clipper. He walked over to a line of rubbish bins and dropped the pieces and the now-dead phone itself into separate containers.

He then resumed his seat, consulted his watch, and laid himself out on the tabletop with his hands behind his head to wait.

Fifteen minutes later a black Lincoln Town Car drove into the parking lot, bumped over the curb, and stopped right beside the picnic table, chewing up grass in the process. The Vespa rider sat up with a jolt.

The Town Car's tinted window rolled down, and an arm emerged with a wad of cash in an outstretched hand. The Vespa rider reached out and took the money, which he then proceeded to count.

"Listen, you fuck," said the person inside the car, waving his exposed arm furiously, "there's your money. Now get the fuck out of town."

The Vespa rider appeared shocked by the accusatory tone, having just done someone a big favor. He raised his hands in a questioning gesture. "What?"

"You don't know, fuckhead? You fucked up."

"I did what?"

"You shot the wrong guy."

"That cannot be. I never miss."

"The wrong fucking guy. You crazy fuck, you shot a fucking cop!"

The Vespa rider turned pale.

"Impossible. You gave me the description, I followed from the man's house."

"Shot a cop! *A cop!*" The man in the car was bouncing up and down in his seat with rage.

"What's this," said the Vespa rider, indicating his fistful of cash, "you're way short. This is not our deal."

"It's what you get for shooting the law. This is trouble for us, so get your ass back to whatever hole you crawled out of, hear me?"

"You owe me money."

"Go ahead and sue, see if we care."

The Vespa rider waved his arms. "Look, I'll give this another tap. How many more guys look like your target?"

"Don't fucking kid me, you fucktard. You're a menace. Get lost. Pronto. Before we all wind up in orange suits."

26

HOURS LATER, after the EMTs and their ambulance departed for the hospital with Voss on a gurney, after a long and tiresome interview with attending police officers was over, Solano, still shaken, caught a taxi to the Silverlode.

He stood facing the main entrance on Virginia Street for a while, marshaling his resolve. Then, with a deep breath, he slipped through the revolving door and navigated through the glitzy sights and sounds of sinful games to the classy ambience of the sports book.

"Hey, Sparkles, I got some more long shots for you."

The book manager took the bets, shaking his head at every one.

Solano turned to leave and stopped cold. Ed Barber was striding toward him, all smiles. The casino manager attempted a big hug, but settled for a vigorous handshake when Solano cringed.

"Here I am," said Solano trying to conceal his ice-cold anger, "losing money on ridiculous spreads."

"And you're doing a great job, Mickey. Great job. Major asset to our operation."

"Unh-huh. Is that right? Not what I hear around town."

"No? Who said such a thing?"

"Doesn't matter. I don't really listen."

"That's good. You shouldn't. We've got a terrific business arrangement going. We're a team."

Solano's face twisted into an ironic grin. The conversation was headed for dangerous subjects, but Solano was a gambler, and although he was inwardly shaking, he was also furious, and his sixth sense told him he was on the right track. He decided to be brave.

"Business. Yup. Like any good businessman I keep my books in shape, Mr. Barber. Also a diary. My accountant has advised me to provide him with copies of everything. You know, *for the record.*"

Barber's jocular attitude visibly cooled.

"There's no need for that, Mickey. Don't be paranoid."

"You heard about the shooting this afternoon, right?" Solano cupped his hands behind both ears to emphasize the question.

"Afraid not. Shooting?"

"I was standing right beside the guy when he went down."

"Goodness gracious," said Barber. "That was close. I'm surely glad to see you on your feet in one piece."

Solano thought it possible that Barber wasn't lying; that the attack originated lower on the executive chain of command.

"Of course you are," Solano said, using a reassuring tone that he knew rang false. "You wouldn't want anything bad to hurt our terrific business arrangement, would you?"

Barber regarded the young gambler through narrowed eyes. Not quite as naïve as he originally thought. He cursed himself for underestimating the guy.

"No, Mickey," he said at last, recalibrating his character assessment, "I would not. And, given your splendid success, I think it's time to award a little raise, up your compensation. How does that sound?"

"It's a start."

27

JAQUOYA CASSIDY, a Nevada Gaming Control Board investigator, having just finished a training session in Las Vegas, was hiking through McCarran International Airport when a call buzzed her mobile phone.

"Yo, Captain. Yes, the session is over. No prob, I graduated head of the class. On my way home now."

She stopped in the middle of the aisle, stunned by news from the other end of the line.

"When did this happen?"

Pause.

"Is he okay? Well, he's going to be, I mean, right?"

Pause.

"Where did they put him?"

Pause.

"Good God."

Pause.

"I know, I know. Thanks for the heads up."

She dropped the phone into her bag, studied the signs for newsstands and restaurants, and steered herself into the Jackpot Lounge for a stiff drink.

There was one other person at the bar, a middle-aged man with sharp features and sandy hair wearing a black nylon jacket. She nodded as she ordered a glass of white wine.

The man knocked back a shot of reposado tequila and studied the newcomer. What he saw was a buxom young woman of indeterminate heritage in a business suit; athletically curvy and very good-looking. He wondered about the meaning of the silver-tipped dreadlocks running back over the middle of her head.

"How ya doin'?" he said.

Cassidy looked directly at the man for the first time. He seemed like an ordinary Joe, but she noticed a melancholy aura radiating from his slumped posture and unfocused eyes.

"Not bad," she replied.

Her drink arrived. She raised the glass. "Here's to on-time flights."

"Whoa, second that," returned the man. "Where you headed?"

"Reno. Home. You?"

"Orlando."

"Business trip?"

The man pressed his lips together and waggled his head. "Yeah, business. Gotta love it."

Cassidy couldn't tell if the man was depressed after failing to close a deal or just didn't care.

"Not a big win, huh?"

The man turned his eyes from his glass to Cassidy. "I missed an easy sale."

"It happens," said Cassidy, being politely sympathetic.

"Not to me."

The man waved to the bartender and ordered up another shot of tequila.

"How about you," he said. "What's your crime?"

Something about the man and his question produced a blip on Cassidy's police radar. She could not put her finger on it, but a caution flag popped up in her head. She thought it best not to talk about cops.

"Training program. Boring stuff I already know all about."

"What's that?"

"Um, record keeping on our new computer system. Customer invoices, that kind of thing. Company ordered me to attend." She pointed at her glass. "Hence this."

"Unh-huh. The modern world. Everybody's got orders. But I'm a freelance guy. A contractor. Nobody tells me what to do."

"Must be a great way to work."

"I do okay. But not today. Today I missed. Shit."

"What are you selling, if I may ask?" said Cassidy, starting to wonder about the man's credentials.

"Selling? Oh, security. Clients get in trouble, they get a whistle-blower or a leaker of corporate secrets, and I consult, suggest ways to reduce risk."

"Sounds exotic."

"Very. Not many people work my field."

"Unh-huh. Do your suggestions get results?"

"Pretty much guaranteed. The leakers and the crazies, the bleeding hearts, the thieves . . . " he let the thought hang, hazily becoming aware that he was talking too much.

"Thieves . . ? What . . ?" Cassidy smiled the winning smile of innocent curiosity.

"Hah!" — he swallowed his shot of tequila — "they lose all desire to talk to reporters, to steal, to blow their whistles, whatever."

"Gotta stop those leakers — sounds like you've got a great product."

"Persuasion. It's a service. A unique service."

"Client here in Vegas?"

"Nahh, Reno. But there's no direct flight to my part of the world this afternoon." He raised his glass. "Like you said, hence this."

Cassidy nodded and turned her attention back to her own drink. After a sip, she decided to probe a little further.

"What kind of persuasion works best? I'd like to persuade my boss sometimes, you know?"

The man placed a hand on his knee and leaned toward her. His eyes were bloodshot. His nose was red. He had downed a couple of shots while she was there to watch, but he obviously had a big head start before she arrived.

"You don't want to know, Miss . . . Trainer Person . . . it's not pretty like you."

His hand slipped off his knee. His head drooped, and his nose touched the bar.

"Whoa, there, mister. You okay?"

The man struggled to resume an upright pose. "I'm . . . hammered, I guess. Missed sale, drowning my sorrows, eck."

Cassidy was picking up a very odd vibe. She excused herself to find the women's restroom, stepped into the hall, and thumbed a button on her mobile phone.

"Hey, Captain, it's me. Still at the Vegas airport. Tell me again, how did the Voss shooting go down?"

Pause.

"He was with this guy Solano, and you think Solano was the target?"

Pause.

"Oh, Solano . . . *the target* thinks he was the target."

Pause.

"Well, was he? Was it a hit that went wrong?"

Keeping an eye on the bar, she walked across the concourse and ducked into the nearest airport news stand.

"Okay, listen to me — here's a scoop. Big. Can't be sure, but I think I've got your hitter sitting beside me at the bar. He's waiting for a flight to Orlando."

Cassidy pulled the phone away from her ear to dampen a flurry of loudly expressed doubts.

"Calm down. I know, what are the chances? But, hey, the Big Guy upstairs doesn't care what we think makes sense."

Pause.

"Maybe I'm wrong, but this man is not right. He's drunk. He told me he's in the security business, persuading leakers not to leak, by means I don't want to know about. He just flew down here from Reno after he — quote — *missed a sale* — unquote. So if I'm imagining things — what? — it's false arrest at worst, we apologize, and I will buy your meals for a week."

Pause.

"Yeah, okay, plus a bottle of scotch and a pile of chips at the Peppermill."

Pause.

"Right, then. I'm on it. How is Luke?"

Pause.

"Unh-huh, fingers crossed."

She ended the call and was starting another one when a uniformed Transportation Security agent walked into the shop to buy a newspaper. Cassidy tugged at the cop's shirt.

"Hey, there, officer," — she flashed her Gaming Control Board badge — "have I got a tip for *you.*"

Ten minutes later three Las Vegas policemen were escorting Cassidy's drunken acquaintance down the concourse. The man was in handcuffs, riding behind a porter on an electric cart, with a cop marching along each side. She watched them go, not sure whether to be proud of herself or worried that she had just caused an innocent man to miss his flight.

28

OFFICER LUKE VOSS was in a semi-private room in the Re-nown Regional Medical Center, not far from where he was shot. There were tubes up his nose, an IV drip in his arm, and a tangle of wires leading to a Dinamap medical monitor from sensors glued to his neck, chest, and a fingertip. The wiggly lines on the screen showed a strong heartbeat and normal blood oxygen. They attested to the quick wits of the emergency responders and to the skill of the surgeons that removed the hitter's bullet and sealed up his punctured lung.

Following a tentative knock on the door, Solano eased quietly into the room, mindful of the patient's delicate condition. The wounded officer was lying on his back in dim light with his eyes closed.

"Hey there, Voss," he whispered. "How's it going?" A conventional greeting, and it was obvious that things could be going a lot better, but Solano couldn't think of anything else to say.

Voss, heavily medicated with opiates and barely conscious, cracked open an eye.

"Solano . . ." His voice was a croak, his speech slurred. ". . . I hurt like hell."

"Yeah," Solano chuckled. "Better you than me."

The sardonic barb caused Voss to lift his head off the pillow, get an elbow under his healthy side. "Who let you in?" he mumbled.

"Your superiors decided the hero of the day deserved a visit."

"Hero?"

"I stopped the bleeding."

"Oh yeah, thanks, I guess."

"What else was I going to do?"

"How do I know you weren't trying to kill me, stop my investigation?" wheezed Voss.

"That's really good. Think — who pops a cop? I was the target."

"Mmm . . . who would want to hit you?"

"Who do you think?"

"Silverlode did this?"

"Who else? You probably scared them into action."

"Damn. They are going to hurt worse than I do."

"Let's hope."

"But don't think that gets you off, pal. We're onto your little laundromat."

Another knock on the door interrupted the hushed conversation. In walked a spectacularly curvaceous young woman in a loose white cotton blouse, jeans, and dreads.

"Hi, Luke. Looking good."

Voss raised a hand in greeting. "Ha-ha."

She leaned over and kissed him on the forehead. Then she turned toward his other visitor.

"Who's this?"

Solano gave her a cautious little wave. "It's Mickey Solano. The officer here — friend of yours? — took a shot meant for me. I just dropped by to thank him."

Voss pointed at her. "Solano, meet Jaquoya Cassidy. She's a cop like me. And now, with these damn tubes and all, she's your new nightmare."

"Solano . . ?" Cassidy stuck out her hand. Solano shook it.

"Whatever he says, I'm innocent."

He smiled. She looked him over and smiled back.

"Excuse us, please," she said. "Luke and I have to plot your downfall."

Solano nodded. "Get well, Voss, and hey, you two — just ignore me."

Once Solano was out of the room, Cassidy laid out her encounter with Voss' probable hitter.

"Turns out our suspect is one Julius Aptekar, a contractor from Orlando, Florida. Originally from — get this — Slovenia, but now a citizen."

"Welcome to America, land of free enterprise," griped Voss.

"Incriminating stuff in his pockets and briefcase, including a big wad of cash."

"His payoff," said Voss.

"Oh yeah. Likely weapon in his checked luggage, along with a Florida carry permit. We'll test for recent firing. I understand we have the bullet that knocked you down."

Voss wondered about Solano. They agreed that he would never have appeared on anyone's hit list unless he knew something about illegal activity, or, more likely, that he was actually in on the crimes.

"Hero or not, your job is to nail that guy," said Voss emphatically. The effort caused him to flop back down on the bed and set off all the alarms on his medical monitor.

"Hey, Luke, you're alive. Show some gratitude," said Cassidy.

▼

Solano left the hospital building and was walking across the parking lot toward his Range Rover when a voice calling from behind caused him to turn around.

"Hey, Mighty Hero, wait up."

He stopped. Jaquoya Cassidy was striding toward him with a big smile on her lips. She closed the gap.

"So, our hitter wasn't after Luke. It was you."

"Mistaken identity, right? We were dressed a lot alike. Same age, same height." Solano shrugged. "It's obvious."

"Not to me. Who doesn't like you?"

"The Silverlode."

"And why's that?"

"They think I win too much. Maybe they think I talk too much."

"What would you talk about? What makes them the bad guys?"

Solano studied the woman. She had those three dreadlocks, but her skin was almost as pale as his. She was smiling seductively, and he sensed she was consciously using her looks to disarm him.

"Here's the thing — I'm a professional. Gambling? It's my life."

"You're good at it, huh?"

"Yes I am."

He resumed walking. She followed half a step behind.

"All the gamblers I ever met were losers," she said. "But not you."

He wasn't fooled by her apparent curiosity, but he couldn't help admiring her act.

"I do okay."

"How? You must be one of those advantage players."

"Of course."

"Card counter? Dice influencer? Roulette ballistics?"

Solano grinned. "None of the above."

"But you cheat, right?"

"Strictly sports, honest bets, all legal . . . and the occasional pathetic slot machine."

She snorted amiably. "You can't win at slots without cheating."

They arrived at his car. To signal the end of their conversation he clicked his key fob. The Range Rover beeped. Lights blinked. He opened the door.

"You going to arrest me?" He smiled as if humoring a socially backward kid.

She angled her head, gauging him. "You don't look like a cheater, I'll give you that."

"Whoa. Flattery. Is this a cop trick?"

She flashed her big smile again. This time it seemed real.

"I'll save the cuffs for another day."

▼

Goldfield's Pub & Pawn was a cozy downtown bar attached to a real if mostly ornamental pawn shop. It had only been open for a couple of years, and the proprietors deliberately designed it to recall an earlier, sleazier Reno. Flanking the little wooden tables were rows of one-armed bandits, old-fashioned slot machines whose mechanical reels were decorated with quaint fruit and bar symbols.

Solano threaded his way through a noisy gaggle of customers carrying two frosty pints of beer. He presented one to Cassidy, and sat down across from her.

"Brewed on the premises," he said.

"Mmm," she murmured.

He clinked his glass against hers.

"Here's to justice," he proclaimed stoutly.

She laughed.

"That's a good one. Your only hope is to avoid it."

"Okay, try this — here's to justice, may it miscarry."

"Much better."

She took a big sip.

"I'm coming after you, you know." She pointed a finger at his chest. "Fair warning."

Solano was not disturbed by the announcement, sensing, albeit faintly, other motives.

"But you seem so friendly," he said, with an infectious grin.

A return smile spread across Cassidy's face. "I have my methods."

"Unh-huh. I'm hip."

She put down her beer and leaned across the table.

"Let's say the Silverlode had enough of you, their big winner. They would throw you out, threaten you, list you, maybe beat you up if nothing else worked, but they would never resort to murder. Unless" — she winked — "unless you, Mr. Advantage Player, are involved in their illegal activities, whatever they might be."

"Whatever, right."

"Luke thinks it's money laundering. I do too. Federal crime, could shut them down if they get indicted."

Solano shifted around in his seat. "What a shame that would be."

"So, hey — the attempted hit can only mean one thing — you're a bad guy too."

"Another Al Capone," he said, with a wry grin.

"Charming bad guy, how's that?" she replied.

Solano grunted to note the compliment without accepting it, sipped his beer, rolled defensive thoughts around in his head.

"Look, you want to score a bust? Of course you do, you're a pro. I notice that one of my acquaintances at the Silverlode is claiming to be a paid escort of Senator Ives."

"Yeah?" Cassidy rolled her eyes. "So the esteemed senator has a sleazy side — like you."

"No, no, you don't understand. She was never near the guy. She was paid to make the claim."

"What? Who?"

"The Russians? The Paxton campaign? Some group colluding with shady characters at a shady casino, where, coincidentally, I have made a lot of money."

Cassidy looked blank.

"I have it from the babe herself. You could go after that angle," prompted Solano. "Arrest some of the bad guys without involving me."

"I don't think politics is on the Control Board's agenda," said Cassidy. Her tone conveyed utter disbelief.

Solano toyed with his beer, inwardly fuming.

"Jaquoya, right? That's your name?"

"Sure is."

"Do people call you Jackie?"

"People call me *Jaquoya.*"

"Whoops, got it. Unusual name . . . kind of formal is what I was thinking."

"You're wondering about the dreads, my light skin."

Solano swallowed. "I guess I am."

Cassidy sat back, squinting at her companion. "I'm a mongrel, but I identify as black."

"Here's the deal, *Jaquoya,*" said Solano, affecting exaggerated courtesy, "I've got a wonderful accountant. He does my books, looks after me. Go ahead, subpoena my stuff, you'll see. I'm legit."

"No doubt . . . when your minders aren't telling you what to do."

"I am — *strictly* — right side up. Walking the righteous path."

"You're an excellent liar, Michael."

"Mickey. And listen, I've also got a terrific attorney and enough money to pay him all the way to the Supreme Court."

Cassidy checked her watch.

"We're having such a nice time. Glad we had a chance to talk."

She tossed her head, shaking her dreads. Solano decided to test his suspicion that her attention went beyond routine police work.

"Dinner?" he asked.

"Whoa, it's late. Can't tonight. Call me." Her eyes twinkled. "Or spot me tailing you. Let's see what happens."

Cassidy finished her beer, handed Solano a business card, and left the bar.

Solano remained in his seat. He lit up his throwaway phone and called his accountant.

"Yo, Jake — I think the Gaming dudes are going to subpoena my accounts, tax returns, everything, the bastards. Be nice, but stall as long as possible."

Pause.

"Tell you what — I'll tip you a winner if you fend them off."

▼

Out on the street Solano noticed a guy dressed in greasy coveralls hanging around, checking cars. The man was peering into the windows of his Range Rover as he approached.

Solano fingered the vehicle's key fob. The man jumped back when the horn sounded. He looked sideways at the owner and backed away, hands up in protest.

"Nice car," he said.

"Thanks," replied Solano. "I plan to keep it that way."

"Of course you do, no harm meant, no harm done."

The greasy guy smiled and offered an awkward little salute as he retreated down the sidewalk.

Solano watched him get into an enormous old Cadillac parked in the next block.

He registered the man's odd appearance and behavior without any curiosity. Then he got behind the wheel of his own ride and drove away.

OCTOBER

29

NEWS of the day.

On the KNVR late show, Maggie Morrison and Diego Ramirez were tag-teaming half-hearted attempts to make local news sound thrilling. The season's big forest fire in the uplands near Gold Hill had yet to burn its last acre. Activists were on camera bemoaning the threat to wild horses roaming the area. Road repairs on I-80 would be closing a lane near Boomtown every night for the following week. The cause of the tragic crash during September's Reno Air Races had been tentatively identified as — what else? — pilot error.

Following a commercial break, the program's anchors turned their attention to politics and the contentious race between Senator Ives and his challenger, Conway Paxton.

"What's the latest, Diego? Any sign of civility?" asked Morrison rhetorically.

"'Fraid not, Mags. This campaign is better than any soap opera we've ever broadcast. Instead of *Days of Our Lives,* it's more like *Lies of Our Days.* Listen to this, from candidate Paxton, speaking way over the border in Sacramento, if you can imagine that . . ."

The scene shifted to Paxton holding a rally in Roseville, a Sacramento suburb. "My friends in California, I know you've got a reputation as a liberal state. A state that just *loves* its regulations, right?"

Cheers and some boos greeted this assessment.

"That's probably why your houses cost so much," continued Paxton, "and why you're sending so many people over the border to push up the prices in my state. Well, time to think about things. Time to change. Time to get with the future, loosen up, let people live a little."

The camera in the KNVR studio caught Ramirez shaking his head. "I thought Paxton was running for senate here in Nevada. What about Ives, Maggie? Is he still hanging around where people can vote for him?"

Morrison nodded. "Senator Ives spent the day here in Reno, Diego. Here's some of his appeal to a local veterans' group . . ."

Now Senator Ives took over the screen, warning of the dangers posed by his challenger.

"Folks, it's truth time. Con-man Paxton, my lying opponent, wants you to believe he's on the side of little people, people who have proudly stepped up to serve their country. People like you, soldiers who came home and found jobs scarce and money tight. People who could use some help. Well, if my opponent wins next month, get ready to starve and die. All forms of public assistance, things you need, will be cut off. Medical care will vanish like a dry lake mirage."

Growls and grumbles from the senator's listeners.

"But I won't let that happen. I won't let a man who wasn't born here, didn't live here until he decided to run for office, and a man who likes to campaign over in his native state more than here with the folks who matter . . . *ruin our lives!*" Ives' face was turning red. He jabbed a finger into the air and placed a hand over his heart. "I've been standing up for Nevada for two decades, and I'll be standing up for Nevada until they plant me."

Morrison appeared in front of continuing footage of the fulminating senator. She gestured toward the now silenced video. "What's the upshot, Diego? Do these speeches make any difference? What do the polls say?"

"Good question, Margaret. The polls show a tight race. First Ives is up a point or two, then Paxton. It's day to day."

"We'll have to wait for the final poll to figure it all out, I guess, huh?" concluded Morrison. "The one that counts, just about a month from now."

"That should end the suspense," agreed Ramirez. He grinned. "And stop us from boring our audience with politics for a while."

30

UP ON LAKE TAHOE, six-thousand feet above sea level, the chill and fog of an Indian summer morning gave way to afternoon sunshine. Solano had driven up from the city in the early hours. Now he was out on the water in a wet suit, sailing his Fanatic windsurfer back and forth across Crystal Bay.

A stiff breeze swelled up, licking the waves into whitecaps. He was bouncing on the chop, every now and then becoming airborne. He did some calculations in his head. One-point-four times the wind-speed on a beam reach. Over twenty miles an hour, at the least, he figured. On a good gust, maybe thirty.

"Hallooooo," he sang out, in a state of athletic ecstasy, one with the board, the water, the sun, gambling troubles forgotten.

Some kid drove up beside him on a jet ski. Solano wiggled his toes firmly into the board's foot straps, leaned back, snapped the sail taut, and hauled ass. The jet ski paced him for a quarter mile, then fell behind. He turned toward the driver, took his left arm off the boom for a friendly wave, and suddenly found himself head over heels into the water. His board skittered away with the sail dragging.

The impact had him disoriented, and he came to the surface snurfling and sneezing. The jet ski pulled alongside.

"You okay, Dad?"

Solano nodded. The kid nodded back, twisted his throttle, and shot away. Solano looked around for his board. There it was, drifting nearby. He dogpaddled over and crawled onto the deck. There he blew his nose and burst out laughing. He was drunk on fun.

After lying there for several minutes, he stood up, grasped the boom with both hands and, huffing and puffing, pulled the mast free of the water. He let the sail luff while he caught his breath. Then he aimed for the California shore, tightened his grip on the boom, pulled the sail in tight again, and took off.

Ten minutes later, while tacking back toward Nevada, he spotted someone walking out on his dock while he was still cruising a couple of hundred yards from shore. He felt his chest tighten, felt his breath quicken. Who was it? Voss was in the hospital. The figure he saw was definitely a man, definitely not Cassidy. He shuddered. Oh my God, another Silverlode hitter?

He tacked back and forth away from his property. Soon, down along the eastern shore, he could see the ruins of the house Bill Gaffney was renting back in July. Someone had cleaned up the mess, but the rebuilding process had yet to start.

Looking at the naked foundation made him think about the unknown man on his dock. No details, but the overall impression struck him: tall, overweight, careless posture, careless dress.

Wait a minute.

He came about and performed a slow broad reach back toward his house.

As he approached the man waved.

Solano pulled up to the dock, maneuvered between his speedboat and his WaveRunner, dropped the sail, and fetched up against the rubber bumpers positioned along the edge. The man leaned down and held the board as Solano stepped off.

"Hi, Mickey, how's it going?"

Solano looked him up and down.

"Gaffney!"

Indeed. The man was tall, overweight, and slouching negligently in a Batman T-shirt and plaid shorts. He made a little bow. Solano shook his head in wonderment.

"You're dead, bro. I saw the ashes."

31

GAFFNEY AND SOLANO were in Solano's Lake Tahoe office drinking beer and staring at computer code they didn't understand.

"What is this crap, Bill?"

"I don't know. It's obfuscated."

"As if I couldn't tell. *Atomic Eff-ing Redstone?* — give me a break."

"The language? Frank's idea. Bulletproof, military qualified, and no one would ever figure out what we were up to."

"Sure, the source is disguised, but the binary, that's gotta be clean so it can run."

"*Au contraire,* dude. That's the beauty part — it's obfuscated at the binary level. Functions are first-class, they don't have dependencies, the calls go through a blockchain, like Bitcoin transactions."

"Tell me you're making this up."

Gaffney shrugged apologetically. "Frank wrote most of the stuff, I just did the decoration. I'm a faded C++ guy, I can't even understand my own code after three months." He grinned. "That's why I gave it to you, champ."

Solano groaned.

"That's just great. So I read up, okay? The decrypt program is supposed to be located in something called obtuse-dot-what-the-hell. You didn't capture that file."

Gaffney thought about the problem.

"I stole everything."

"Not quite, it seems."

"Everything, bro."

Solano raised his hands in mock surrender.

Gaffney thought some more. He removed his Mario-themed baseball cap and ran a frustrated hand through his long hair. "It's gotta be here, a hidden file."

"My hidden files are all turned on."

"Can't be," insisted Gaffney. "No, no, no. I bet you're still hiding the protected OS files."

Solano let out an exasperated sigh. "I'll check."

He wasn't expecting results, but hey, when the file options dialogue box appeared, there was a check mark indicating that the operating system files remained hidden. Solano unchecked the mark.

"Tah-dah!" said Gaffney, pointing at the window listing the MicroSD card files. The missing item was now on view:

```
obtuse.sys
```

Solano opened it up.

"Oh, crap," he said. They were staring at completely incomprehensible gibberish:

```
Bd>u$¶5x!7#*vv>c2a%^:áoR#DfpXcI63EBHoHW@^6+]!è§<
<†777dê‡48=8<9o%3*\F\39EL4#5^6&\nPi2>:@§KSPR÷u$¶
zR6y3w2<£<!!+f:L|>|t$•‡00*?0^#5%¶?•Rv§<55:rt:[UI
```

The apparent nonsense went on forever. Gaffney swigged his beer. Then, "Got it!" he announced. "That mess isn't obfuscation, it's actual code seen as text. We just need to change the file type, make it an executable."

Solano duly altered the file name:

```
obtuse.exe
```

He clicked on the result. His computer display turned black, with a message floating near the top:

```
WHO DARES DISTURB MY SLUMBER?
```

"Oh wonderful," mumbled Solano, "that's so cute."

"Try *Osgood*," prompted Gaffney. "All caps."

Solano wrote the dead programmer's name. A new message appeared:

CAN YOU SAY THE MAGIC WORD?

"Uh-oh," said Solano. "Abracadabra?"

"Doubt it," replied Gaffney unhelpfully.

"Well? You're the Patriotic guy. Give me something here."

Gaffney shook his head. "Frank never told me his password."

"What about his birthday, phone number, mailing address, mother, favorite pet, sports hero, best friend?"

"He was kind of private, when I think back. I don't have a clue."

"Then we are hosed."

"Actually," mused Gaffney, "if you want to know the truth, Frank was a stuck up, holier-than-thou, prissy little shit. He wouldn't tell me anything I didn't need to know. Try *patriotic.*"

Solano typed the name and got a new message for his trouble:

NONE SHALL PASS

"Damn."

Solano rose from his seat and retrieved a couple of Mountain Dews from his refrigerator. Jolts of caffeine to counteract the beer. He handed one to Gaffney.

"Let's think this through."

"Right, thinking."

They drank in silence for a while.

"My internal suggestion box is empty, Mick."

"Yeah, me too."

Another silence. Solano emptied his soda in three gulps and changed the subject.

"So . . . what's it like to be dead?"

Gaffney rolled his shoulders uneasily. He shivered. "I'm a ghost of myself. I was next, bro. Now I can stay out of sight."

"Who belonged to the ashes impersonating you?"

"I didn't know there were ashes until you told me. So, my guess is — the same guy who killed Frank was after me, and — whoops! —

he made a big mistake."

"Hired by Patriotic?"

"Who knows? I never went in the house. When I got there, lights were on. I could see someone's shadow on the window. I pushed my bike three blocks before I dared to fire it up."

"You saw a shadow."

"Spooky. And if that shadow didn't report for work next day, the bad guys may not think I'm dead. Why I'm flying low."

"What about your friends? What did you tell them?"

"I have no friends. None. Except you, Mick."

"Unh-huh. We need that password," said Solano.

"And I need a snack," said Gaffney. "Got any pizza?" He shambled into the kitchen.

▼

An hour later, the pair still hadn't discovered the password. Solano was brooding. "Osgood, a prissy little shit — that's what you said, right?"

Gaffney scratched his head. "I'll say. Maybe my plan won't work."

"Plan?"

"We crack the code, go to the authorities, and make damn sure nobody relies on fucking Patriotic for an honest vote count this fall."

"Not looking good, chief," said Solano wearily.

"But there's still my backup plan," declared Gaffney. "No way will that fuck Paxton become senator from Nevada."

Solano was unprepared for Gaffney's casual belligerence. "Wait a sec. The election looks like a close call. How do we know it's not three-term Senator Ives who wants a boost?"

"Are you kidding? That old fart is *ethical*. Way too twentieth century."

"All right then, Paxton it is . . . backup plan?"

"Oh, I've got one, don't worry."

"Tell me."

"No way, Mick. You don't need to know."

"Oh, for Pete's sake."

"Nope, gotta play some cards close to the vest. You know all about that."

"I never play cards," retorted Solano. He was considering the imagined psychology of the dead programmer.

"Would you say Osgood was egotistical?"

Gaffney chuckled. "In spades."

Solano typed a password:

OHSOGOOD

He let out a yell and clapped his hands. "I changed two letters! Have a look at that, Billy Backup. Here we have Plan A —"

ENTER THE CHAMBER, CHOSEN ONE

They bumped fists. Solano clicked on the message and received another one:

ALL KNOWLEDGE TO THE PRINCE OF ELVENDOM

Gaffney was suddenly excited. "I am the prince, you are the king! Look at the other files, bro."

Solano duly opened the file *newfunctionbin.red.* Now they were looking at a different kind of mystery:

```
<< :blk4: put {zero <r> enm;} into vlst; sort
(vlst) {order high;} put (result) into {assemble
proof;} from proof >> :blk6: call krypt; try con-
firm (k66) {<r> vlst;} catch (nokryp) {flush error
into manout;} confirm (proof) {vlst <r> vlst_mir-
ror;} >> :blk4: proof++; vlst++; rtn >> :blk6:;
```

"This is as bad as before. I see words, but I don't understand them," moaned Solano. "This stuff does something?"

"Oh yeah, man, you better believe. It runs the whole machine," said Gaffney. Then, as an afterthought, "well . . . somehow."

Solano scowled. "How many lines of code, anyway?"

"I dunno, a million or two. It's tight, compact."

"Right, very compact," mumbled Solano.

"Hang in there, king, we're almost done," said Gaffney.
He crossed the room, laid himself down on Solano's sofa, and was asleep in seconds.

Solano stood up, flexed his muscles, and arched his back, which was sore. He looked out through one of his huge picture windows at the lake. Light was fading. The planet Venus was visible above the western mountains.

"Trixie, play that foothill radio station," he commanded. "I like their stuff."

"Will do, Mickey," replied the audiobot. "Here's K-V-I-G."

The tail end of an alternative rock song welled up on Solano's built-in speaker system.

"Hello, out there," said the disc jockey in mellifluous tones. "This is the Golden Girl of the Golden Hills, in Applefield, California. Tonight I'm taking none but the best of requests. And now, for you folks who were partying a little too hearty on Upper Bar Lake this afternoon, here's Harry Nilsson . . ."

The Coconut Song blasted into the room.

Solano sat back down and stared at the code on his screen.

"Put the name in the function call, confirm the proof of vee-list," he sang, head wagging to the music. *"Put the proof in the krypt, and call me in the morning."*

He ran down through the long lines of code, marveling at the obscurity of the Redstone computer language.

"Trixie, coffee, please."

"Friends don't let friends drive drunk," warbled the audiobot, possibly confused by the odd hour.

"Not drunk, just tired. And depressed. Getting nowhere."

"That's nice, Mickey. Good to hear. Coffee in three minutes."

▼

Several hours later Solano gave up. The sky was showing color, and soon the morning sun would swing up above the eastern shore of Lake Tahoe and turn its dark gray water brilliant blue.

"Man, I'm whipped," he said aloud.

His voice woke Gaffney. The big man rubbed his head, rubbed his eyes. He shuffled over to Solano's computer and stared at the blank screen.

"You crack it, bro?" he wondered.

"Not a chance," said Solano glumly.

Gaffney looked out the window. "Damn, I have to split, before the spies show up."

"Spies?"

"They're everywhere, Mick. The KGB, Paxton and his crew, the military-industrial takeover."

Solano shrugged the indifference of the damned. "Right, they'll be here any minute. What the *fuck* are you talking about?"

Gaffney wiggled his eyebrows. "It's real, bro. Don't tell them anything."

Before Solano could ask for clarification, Gaffney had the front door open and was heading for his ride, a Honda motorcycle.

"How will I find you — hey? — Bill? — Wanna tell me?"

"No worries. You will crack the code, and I will find *you.*"

With that, Solano's visitor cranked the starter on his bike, revved the engine, and roared away toward Reno.

32

SOLANO SLEPT through the morning hours. Then he showered, put on clean clothes, slipped into his Range Rover, and headed for the city, up and over the Mount Rose Summit at nine thousand feet, and down the long grade into the Washoe Basin.

On the way he fished Jaquoya Cassidy's business card from a pocket and made a hands-free call to her direct line at the Gaming Control Board. She did not pick up, and her voicemail alert chirped.

"Hello, Ms. Cassidy. It's Mickey Solano. When can we get together? We've got a lot to talk about."

He ended the call, chuckling over his cryptic message. "That ought to get your attention. Sounds like a confession coming, right? Hah! Guess again, Law Lady."

When he reached the intersection of the Mount Rose Highway and Interstate 580, he turned north toward downtown Reno. Then, on a whim, he steered onto the freeway exit at Meadows Parkway, miles short of the city center.

The Reno office of the Nevada Gaming Control Board was located in a warren of newly erected office buildings on the southern edge of the city, where rents and construction costs were low, and where concrete tilt-up structures were what passed for modern style.

Solano pulled into the parking lot and maneuvered into an empty space near the Control Board entrance. He was in the middle of his second call to Cassidy when the officer herself appeared, chatting with another woman. She was wearing a linen pant suit over a pale blue blouse.

Solano stepped out of his SUV and touched his key fob. The Range Rover's lights blinked, and its horn emitted a well-mannered bleat. Cassidy looked up. Solano waved.

Cassidy threw up her hands, excused herself, and marched across the lot to Solano.

"What's up, Mickey High Roller?"

Solano grimaced. He indicated his watch. "It's like twelve-thirty. Lunch?"

Cassidy raised her arms helplessly in the direction of the woman she was with. The woman grinned, waved cheerfully, and disappeared into a little Toyota.

"Okay, change of plans." She removed the ID card hanging around her neck and stuffed it into a jacket pocket. "Where to? You're buying."

▼

On the outside deck of the Turquoise Tavern, under the shade of its wide umbrellas, Solano and Cassidy ordered lunch from a gay young waiter. A pastrami sandwich and beer for Solano, red pepper omelet and coffee for Cassidy. While they waited for their food, Cassidy idly stirred cream and Splenda into her cup.

"Solano. What kind of name is that?" she wondered.

"Hispanic, of course."

"Mexico?"

"Cuba. My grandfather was one of the *gusanos* fleeing the Castro regime. He wound up in Vegas. But Dad married an Irish girl."

"So, you're a mongrel like me."

"America the Beautiful."

"Amen," said Cassidy. She touched her cup against Solano's glass.

Their food arrived, interrupting the conversation. After a few moments with knives and forks and napkins, Cassidy appraised her lunch companion through narrow eyes.

"So, Mickey, why are we here? I heard some voicemail. Ready to come clean?"

Solano leaned forward. He smiled. "Boy, you never let up. I am clean. I'm also small fry. But election fraud — that's big."

He launched into his litany of complaints about the possibility of Russian election meddling, the Paxton campaign, Frank Osgood, the murdered Patriotic coder, and Jenny Penny's paid escort charade.

"That's something for Channel Four. You should tell them."

"I tried. They don't seem interested. That's why I'm telling you."

"Trying to distract me, you mean."

Solano attempted to conceal his exasperation with another thought, all about his friend who was killed in an explosive house fire.

"Accidents happen," she said.

"But my friend didn't burn up. He's still alive."

"Your point . . ?"

"I saw the remains. A skull, some bones, ashes. So someone got caught in the blaze. I think the guy was from the Silverlode, helping somebody cover up their fraud scheme. Maybe he's the guy who knocked off Frank Osgood."

"You are being very paranoid, Mickey. Why on Earth would the Silverlode get involved with election fraud? It doesn't make sense."

Solano rolled his eyes. "I thought you were a cop. Law and order, protect and serve, suspicious about everything, not just me."

Cassidy wrinkled her nose. "Perfect description of my very self."

"Well then — I think Paxton's people hired a woman to smear Ives. That woman is a Silverlode employee. Check, why don't you, if another employee stopped showing up for work about a month ago, *comprende?*"

Cassidy forked the remains of her omelet to the side of her plate. "I might do that."

Solano was determined to drive home his working hypothesis. "The Silverlode is old-school. No doubt they cook their books. Dick Worden would be happy to break legs. Probably has. Paxton's campaign is crooked, but they wouldn't know how to play dirty tricks or erase a witness, so they hired a team who does. The Silverlode. Take them out and I'm a free man."

Cassidy sat through the lecture with furrowed brow. "Oh no. You're just a crooked gambler trying to weasel out of trouble with your oily charm."

▼

"Oily?" queried Solano as they left the restaurant. He was offended by the accusation.

Cassidy laughed lightly, but did not retract her assessment. They continued along the sidewalk, heading for their cars. Solano came to a halt outside the main entrance to The Desert Caravan, a small downtown gambling hall catering to locals.

"You think I got rich by laundering money," he said. "Come on, I'll show you how it really works."

He led the way into the dimly-lit casino, an establishment that had seen better days. The aroma of spilled beer vied with stale cigarette smoke and the glare of old-time racer lights for ambience. Twangy country music was playing on dusty loudspeakers overhead.

"What are we doing?"

Solano pointed at a row of video slot machines, each one glittering with multicolored LEDs, in stark contrast to the room's background décor.

"First we watch."

"Okay, watching."

The vigil went on for a while.

"Listen, Mickey. When I found out you were being dragged in for questioning by my sometime partner Luke, I checked you out. You used to work for one of the video gaming companies here in Reno."

"HighScore."

"Right. Those guys. So you launder money, and you've also got some way to cheat their machines we haven't figured out yet."

"I never touch HighScore slots," said Solano. He inserted a credit card into a convenient ticket printer and received a slip of paper worth fifty bucks. He handed it to Cassidy.

"See that woman playing the *Queen of Egypt?* "She just lost like ten spins in a row. Now she's going to quit. Too bad for her. When she does, take her place."

"What?"

Sure enough, the woman let out a heavy sigh, pulled her ticket, and left her seat. Cassidy just stood staring until Solano pushed her into the chair.

"Insert ticket. You do work for the Gaming Control Board, right? You know the drill?"

Cassidy inserted the slip of paper into the ticket slot.

"Now press *Spin.*"

"Now?"

"Right now."

Cassidy pressed the *Spin* button. The video reels whirled madly and settled with three mummy icons on the payline. Lights flashed.

"Again."

Cassidy pressed the *Spin* button again. This time she saw an ankh, an Anubis head, and a pyramid on the payline. No lights.

"Again."

Three Anubis heads signaled another round of flashing lights and flute-like bleeps.

"Go, go."

Cassidy jabbed at the button and was rewarded with three ankhs. A cascade of lights went off like Fourth of July fireworks.

She kept spinning and winning. Pyramids, pharaohs, the Queen herself, each one worth more than the last.

"Okay, Jaquoya. Time to quit."

By now Cassidy was completely absorbed in the game. "Not yet, I'm up five hundred bucks."

She spun again. A chariot, a boat, and the ancient god Set commandeered the payline.

"Damn," she muttered.

"Now you're only up four-fifty. I warned you." He reached past her shoulder and pushed the *Cash Out* button.

At the cashier's window, Cassidy exchanged her ticket for four hundred and fifty dollars.

Back outside, she waved the bills as she opened her purse.

"That was cool. Lady Luck sure likes you."

"Luck doesn't have much to do with it. I sense the patterns."

"Oh, right, it's your superpower," scoffed Cassidy.

"You saw the result. Keep at it and the coins rack up. That's how I do what I do."

"You have — what? — a sixth sense?"

"Exactly!"

Cassidy regarded Solano skeptically. He looked like he was telling the truth. He looked like an honest Joe. His demonstration was impressive . . . but she was not persuaded.

"All right, maybe you know how to win. Well, know this — I still think you're a crook. Eventually I'll have your ass."

Solano shook his head. He grinned. "Literally or figuratively?"

Cassidy giggled, charmed by the man in spite of herself. *"That* depends on how you play your cards."

Solano considered the very bold policewoman. He thought she might be a future opportunity, but at the moment she looked like a trap.

"I never play cards. Drive you to your car?"

"That's okay. I'll walk."

33

AN AUTUMN MORNING on Lake Tahoe.

Wisps of fog were swirling over chilly water. The summer's fleet of boats had thinned out along with the crowds of vacationers.

Solano was at his office desk, staring out a window at the *Tahoe Gal,* a faux side-wheel paddle boat chugging along the California shore near Tahoe City with a few die-hard tourists aboard.

He had spent half a restless night working on voting machine code, and when that didn't produce results, the other half investigating election fraud by googling the Paxton campaign and every news story about it. He was daydreaming about better outcomes with drooping eyelids when there came a loud knock on his door.

He checked his surveillance camera. Bill Gaffney was standing on his little patio. The man's motorcycle was carefully concealed behind Solano's front yard fence.

"Trixie, unlock the front door."

Gaffney shuffled into Solano's office dragging a heavy backpack. "Morning, Mick. I lost them."

"Lost who?" replied Solano.

"Them," Gaffney declared, with a face long enough to announce a Russian invasion.

"Oh, right, the spies."

"Dark blue Chrysler 300. It was on my tail all the way up the grade. But I pulled away in the switchbacks."

"Good for you. Whatcha got there?"

Gaffney lifted a long black tube out of the pack. He hooked it up to a pair of circular mounting brackets with heavy rubber bands and fastened the combination to a tripod.

"This, my friend, is a laser mike. Infrared, no can see the beam. It will pick up any voice vibrating a closed window up to a quarter of a mile away."

"It looks like a ray gun," said Solano doubtfully.

Gaffney reached into the pack and brought forth an olive green metal box, a large battery pack wrapped in black canvas, and a tangle of wires and cables.

"And here's my radio transmitter. It uses this mega-fizz lithium battery to send the signal to this . . ."

He removed a slender gray slab from the pack and opened up a multi-pronged antenna the size of a basketball hoop.

". . . the receiver," finished Solano.

"Right. Two meter band. It's a shipping channel."

"Totally illegal, right?"

"Totally. But I figure we'll be using it in Vegas. No ships anywhere near us, and we won't be on the air too long."

"We . . ?"

Gaffney stood up proud and tall. He puffed out his chest. "We, brother Solano, are going to spray a can of surveillance on the bad guys. Get a confession."

"We are?" Solano was dumbfounded by the idea. "How? Where?"

Gaffney's shoulders slumped. "Got any coffee?"

"Unh-huh. But first, some details? What's the big idea?"

Gaffney pursed his lips. He shrugged. "I was thinking Paxton campaign HQ, down in Vegas."

"Why not Moscow?"

Gaffney failed to register the mockery. "The Russians might be involved, they're around, all over the place."

"Mmm."

"But they'll be working through Paxton."

"Naturally."

"So, campaign HQ — gotta be in some office building, right? We can set up in a hotel room across the street or something, point this mother at their window, get an earful."

Solano scowled. This was no plan at all. "Hey, Bill? Hotel windows don't open. And I hate Vegas. Forget it."

"Come on, Mickey. I need you on this."

Solano waved at the electronic gear sitting on the floor. "Where did you buy this pile of crap? War surplus? Are you sure it works?"

"Absolutely."

"You tested it?"

"Sort of. All the lights go on when I flip the switches. It heard me talking to my mirror."

Solano jerked a thumb toward his kitchen. "Coffee's on the counter. Donuts in the box."

While Gaffney was off fueling up, Solano returned to his Google searches. By the time his visitor had finished off a second cup of java and chewed through most of the available pastry, Solano was ready with an idea.

"Here's a possibility — the morning paper, no less an authority than the *Reno Register,* says Paxton himself and his staff are taking a break. A long weekend getaway courtesy of Lloyd Snell."

"Snell? Who's he?" wondered Gaffney, staring over Solano's shoulder at the newspaper's website.

"For a conspiracy nut, you are low on actual conspirators. Snell is a bigtime industrialist, finances all kinds of right-wing causes."

"One-percenter, rolling in dough, enemy of the people type," muttered Gaffney uncertainly.

"Yup. And here's the good part — the getaway is scheduled for Snell's vacation house up at Northstar."

"The ski area."

"Right. Just up the road."

"No snow."

"God Almighty, Bill. They don't want to go skiing."

"Instead, they're holed up plotting their plots," nodded Gaffney, catching on slowly.

Solano stood up from his desk. He hefted the laser mike, examined the radio transmitter. His thoughts turned to Gigi Newhouse, how she was eager at first, then willing to give up so easily. He rebelled against her casual passivity. Not his style, he reminded himself.

"What the hell," he said, resigned to the challenge in spite of his strong sense that the probability of success was very, very low.

"Problem?" queried Gaffney.

"No, no, not at all." Solano rubbed his eyes. He cleared his throat. "Here's my thought — in the off-season, Northstar doubles as a mountain bike attraction. You ride up the lift with your bike on a hook and then bounce down the ski trails. We could do that and ride down to Snell's place. Avoid the gate in the man's gated community."

Gaffney's eyes lit up. "Perfect. We hide in the trees. The soldiers of Satan blab their nefarious secrets, we collect their evil words and blow our whistles."

"Except we need Snell's actual address," groaned Solano.

▼

Big problem, and it had Solano and Gaffney pacing the floor.

"The only person I know who might have a lead is a woman I met at KNVR," mused Solano.

"Call her, bro," ordered Gaffney, excited by the possibility.

"I might have to." Solano did not relish the prospect.

"Come on, get on it. We need that location."

"It's a hassle. We're not seeing each other anymore."

"So pretend you are. Damn, plead heartbreak or something."

"Ahhh . . . *shit.*" Solano was working himself up to make the call when he remembered the *Register's* online news item.

"Wait, wait, hang on . . ."

He brought up the paper's website in his browser. There he found a link to a KNVR video report.

Solano clicked on the link. After the mind-numbing advertisements ended, he was watching Conway Paxton arrive at a mountainside retreat in a long black limousine. The driver pulled away to reveal Lloyd Snell greeting the candidate with a handshake and a slap on the back.

Gaffney was puzzled. "Why would Paxton let it be known this miserable parasite supports him?"

"No idea," muttered Solano. He pressed *Alt-PrtScr* to grab a screenshot and closed the browser.

"Hey!" yelped Gaffney.

Solano launched a photo-viewing program and opened the screenshot. He zoomed in and panned around the image.

"Look what I found, Billy Boy . . ."

Solano had the frame centered on a rock at the curb in front of the Snell estate. It was painted white, and the number *743* was stenciled on it. A little blurry, but readable.

"Now, landmarks," muttered Solano. He zoomed back out to take in the entire field of view. "There's a cute little guardhouse on the left. White with red and blue stripes. Shelter for a mailbox? Dark green roof on the monster house. Beige walls. Stucco or maybe wood paneling. Big flag flying above the deck there."

"We got him!" cackled Gaffney.

"Not quite. We don't have the street name."

But soon he did. Google Street View showed the fancy development in midwinter snow, but clicking along the curving roads eventually yielded a recognizable view of Snell's palatial mansion. Solano backed up to an intersection and examined the sign.

"Coyote Track Way. Just down the hill from Lookout Lodge."

34

SOLANO AND GAFFNEY arrived at the Northstar Village complex with a pair of rented mountain bikes. Solano thought the resort's own offerings would be impossibly heavy junk designed to withstand customer abuse and not much else. As a precaution they detoured into Kings Beach on their way and picked out a couple of high-performance trail models at All Seasons Alpine Adventures.

Halfway through the Village mall, they stopped at Earthly Delights for beers and sandwiches, tucked them into fanny packs, and continued onward to the Big Springs Gondola.

There an attendant lifted the bikes onto pegs welded to the exterior of the glassed-in cars, one for Solano and one for Gaffney, and sent them up the hill.

When they dismounted at Big Springs Lodge, Solano consulted a little paper trail guide. He pointed to the southwest, where the Tahoe Zephyr Express quad chair ski lift was operating. Once again an attendant placed their bikes on pegs, one per chair. When the machines were on their way, Solano and Gaffney hopped aboard a following chair and continued up toward the summit of Mount Pluto, completely denuded of any snow at the end of a long dry summer.

They were now almost eight thousand feet up, riding high over the grassy terrain on a cable, and the air was cool.

"Man, the ground is so rough," noted Gaffney as a biker jouncing down the lift line beneath them went tumbling over his handlebars.

"I'm freezing," said Solano.

"Hang on, Brother. The forces of truth do not complain."

They dismounted at Zephyr Lodge, and Solano again consulted his trail guide.

"This way. Up and over on the grooming track."

All at once they were working hard, churning up steep terrain with their chains on their granny wheels and derailleurs on their lowest gears. Gaffney, big and heavy by himself, was also carrying most of the surveillance gear. He was sweating.

"Jesus, this is murder," he whined.

Solano gritted his teeth. "But the forces of whatever do not complain."

They reached the crest overlooking Mount Pluto's western slopes. In the distant valley beyond they could see stripes of bright green, the Martis Camp golf course.

"Onward!" cried Gaffney and took off down the snowmobile road. Solano followed at a circumspect distance and speed.

Gaffney skidded around the corners, but did not lose control. Soon thereafter they were standing at the upper terminus of the Martis Camp Express, another quad ski lift catering to residents of the fancy development where Snell's vacation digs were located.

"Down there," said Solano. "Lookout Lodge and hook a left."

They started down the lift line, and the going was slow. The ground was hummocky. There were boulders and tree stumps concealed by tall grass. Gaffney fell twice. Solano relieved him of his heavy pack, and they bounced down to the lodge, closed until ski season. They pedaled around the buildings, and suddenly they were riding through a well-maintained asphalt parking lot.

They turned left on Greenleaf Road, flanked by the tall conifers of an open woodland, and worked their way up a gentle grade to Coyote Track Way.

"Okay, Mick, this is it," said Gaffney. He rolled his bike off the road and dropped it out of sight behind a tree. "We've got to hike through the forest here, sneak up on our target."

Solano disagreed. "We need to see the house number. Google didn't show me Snell's back yard."

"Well, crap," grumbled Gaffney.

"Wait here."

Solano remounted his bike and rode along Coyote Track Way to number 743, counting houses. He continued on past, then circled around and rode back to the street's intersection with Greenleaf Road.

"They see you?" worried Gaffney.

"Nope. Snell's mansion is the third house down. Hard to miss." He dragged his bike into the trees and lowered it on top of Gaffney's.

"Let's go."

Keeping well away from the houses, they picked their way through the woods.

"Okay, here we are. Huge footprint, green roof, beige walls." noted Solano.

"And, what do you know? A fence," mumbled Gaffney. He peered through the trees. There was no clear view of the sprawling mansion, but he thought he saw a promising target for his laser microphone — a wide picture window above an even wider deck. He looked up. A towering Douglas-fir loomed right behind him.

"We can set up in this tree here," he said, pointing.

"How do you propose to climb that thing?" growled Solano.

Gaffney looked again. His face fell. The lowest branch was twenty feet above the ground. "I guess not, huh?"

They circled around until they found a much younger and smaller tree with branches sprouting from below head height. A quick check confirmed that Snell's picture window was still in view.

"How are you at climbing?" asked Gaffney.

"Better than you, obviously," noted Solano, observing the queasy look on his friend's face. He started up into the tree.

Gaffney reached into his pack and pulled out the end of a braided climber's rope. "Take this. Then you can haul up the pack."

"How about you?"

"Standing guard for now."

"You have to climb to set up our equipment."

Gaffney nodded sheepishly. "If you don't fall, I'll get up there."

Solano climbed and climbed, using the profusion of branches arranged around the tree trunk as a ladder. Pretty quick he was forty feet up, and Gaffney, standing far below, was almost out of sight under a dense canopy of evergreen needles.

"Can you see the house from up there?"

Solano moved his head around. He broke off a couple of small limbs. "Yes, I see about half of the window you like. Is that enough?"

Gaffney jerked the rope. "Perfect, haul away," he commanded.

Solano hauled Gaffney's pack up to his position hand over hand. He used the loose rope end to lash it to the branch he was sitting on, and freed the laser mike, radio, and battery. He was sweating.

"Okay, Bill. Up and at 'em!"

But Gaffney made no motion toward the tree. Instead, he was walking away toward Snell's fence line. "Need a minute, bro," he said over his shoulder.

What the hell? Solano pushed twigs and needles out of the way for a good look. Gaffney was striding casually through the trees, whistling a little tune.

"Where do you think you're going, pal?" muttered Solano, worried about being abandoned. Then, suddenly, he understood. A dog was barking. Gaffney stopped and raised his hands. The dog loped through the trees to meet him, sniffed his feet, sniffed his crotch. Gaffney bent down and patted the animal.

"Hey, good doggie."

The dog's keeper, a uniformed security guard with a gun on his belt, was right behind the animal.

"Whoa, there, mister. This is private property, and you, sir, are trespassing."

Solano caught his breath, imagining that his unreliable friend was getting ready to confess. But no. Gaffney pointed back where he came from.

"Trespassing? Really? I live back over that way, next block. On vacation, renting, first time here on the mountain, out for a stroll, no idea where anything is."

"Well sir, that's fine and dandy, but you've got to move along."

"Oh sure, I'll get right out of your way." Gaffney turned around.

"Sorry, no, can't go back there. Your best bet is keep on to the road and follow it around to your place."

"Right, right, got it. Have a nice day." Gaffney gave the guard a nervous little salute and trudged away.

Solano watched him weave among the loosely spaced trees and disappear. "Goddammit, man. Get your ass back here," he moaned. Then he froze. The guard's dog was moving his way, nose down in the duff, sniffing. And the scent was leading him right to Solano's location.

"Hey, whatcha got, Dingo?" said the guard.

Solano shrank into the greenery, sure that he was about to be discovered, arrested, possibly shot.

The dog looked up, then lifted a leg and peed on the tree trunk.

"Okay, boy, good boy, come here, Ding, gotta get back on the loop."

"Arf!" barked the dog and followed his master back to the fence line.

Solano slowly exhaled. After the guard was well out of sight, he started studying the surveillance equipment. Lots of sockets, plugs, cables, and wires, he noticed. But no instruction manual and no Gaffney.

"Hey, Mick," came a cautious voice fifteen minutes later.

Solano peered down. Gaffney had circled around and was standing at the base of the tree, getting ready to climb up. It took a while, but eventually he joined Solano in the high branches.

"That was pretty cool, Bill, what you did," said Solano.

"For the record, I did not soil my pants."

"I thought you were going to leave me hanging here."

Gaffney looked hurt. "Leave you? No way, brother. That guard, if everything went to hell . . ."

He reached under his shirt and pulled out a very dangerous-looking pistol.

"You bought a *gun?*"

"Damn right. Glock 17. 9mm, semi-automatic, serious firepower. Gotta be prepared."

▼

Gaffney set up his laser mike using Velcro straps to bind its tripod to the tree trunk. He lashed his radio and battery to the tree as well and plugged everything together with long cables. He ran the transmitter antenna wire out along one of the branches and looped it around a dead twig. He sighted the laser mike on the visible portion of Snell's picture window. Finally, he switched on his radio receiver and plugged in an earbud.

"We're hot, bro. Listen to this . . ."

He passed the earbud to Solano. A conversation was underway, and the voices were coming through loud and clear.

"How would you like your margarita, Mr. Paxton?"

"That would be top shelf with mango juice."

"Right away, sir."

"Maybe they'll talk about the Russians," said Gaffney hopefully. "Wouldn't that be cool!"

But the brief exchange was followed by crackling silence.

"Did we lose the signal?"

Gaffney had another listen.

"No, nobody's talking. Maybe they left the room."

"How far away can your little receiver hear this stuff?"

"Got a full wave antenna on the X-mitter unit. All the way to your house?"

"Then let's get the hell out of here."

35

BACK AT SOLANO'S lake house, the two spies were laughing over their exploit and their near discovery by Snell's security patrol.

Between bites of a take-out pizza, Gaffney readied his radio receiver by opening the web-like antenna, running it on a long wire through Solano's kitchen door. He lined it up in the direction of Northstar by propping the thing on a patio chair.

To capture a record of anything they heard, Solano connected the receiver to a tiny digital voice recorder. Gaffney turned everything on, and they sat back to await events.

For a while, nothing but static came through on the airwaves. The pair's lighthearted mood soured.

"Sure that antenna got hooked up okay? Aimed at our target?"

"Sure I'm sure. The ski resort is behind Mount Pluto, northwest of here, right?"

"Right."

"So we wait. Maybe everyone's out in the hot tub."

They waited. A couple of beers and a bag of pretzels later, they were still waiting. But then came the babble of many voices. They were unintelligible, but Solano and Gaffney perked up. After a few moments, although still half-drowned in a sea of crackling and hissing radio static, the voices became more distinct. By concentrating hard, the sense of the conversation could be understood.

▼

Roger Neff, Paxton's campaign manager, a smooth operator in his early forties, had just arrived at Snell's palatial mansion. He was there to brief the wealthy supporter, his political consultant Walter Bascomb, and the candidate himself on the state of the senate race.

The group migrated slowly from the main hall into a rustic salon, where immense timbers framed a wide picture window and the window's superb alpine view.

Drinks were served by household staffers in bright yellow jackets.

"Here's to the new era," said Snell, raising his glass of scotch whisky. "It begins just across the line in Nevada. Our victory will tip the senate. And then . . . on to the next race, wherever that may be."

"Hear, hear!" said the others. Glasses clinked, high fives were exchanged.

"Now, people, here's where we stand today, six weeks from the finish line," said Neff, pulling the meeting together. "We're using the usual voter suppression techniques — negative ads, disparagement, you name it — if it's in the book of dirty tricks, we've read the instructions and put them to work."

More expressions of enthusiasm and satisfaction.

"Now, Conway, you're the best candidate I've ever worked for, terrific campaigner, and we've made great strides together. But the truth is, the race is close, and you still trail in the latest polls."

"What about our paid escort?" asked Bascomb.

"That was a well-dropped bomb, Wally. It blew up in Ives' face, and it bought us — what? — about three points. We need almost three more."

"If it's a question of money, you know you can count on me," promised Snell.

"That's great," nodded Neff, swallowing his drink in one gulp. He lifted his empty glass toward Snell in a grateful salute. "We will probably have to take advantage of more than your fine spirits."

"I'll hit the road wherever you want me," avowed Paxton. "I was thinking we might consider a rally over in Ely, where that old copper mine could reopen if government loosened up the environmental regs."

"Not a bad idea, Conway — lots of folks love Nevada's mining tradition, and it might stir them up."

Bascomb was doubtful. "All of the above. Do it all. But remember our demographics. The campaign will narrow the margin, we hope, but Ives will take Las Vegas. The rest of the state will go for us, but the population is thin, votes few. That leaves Reno, always a swing city. That's where Mr. Snell's plan comes into force."

"Plan? What plan is that?" wondered Neff, completely mystified by the claim.

"It's really Wally's brainchild," purred Snell with a sly smile. "But I have helped in the implementation."

"What are we talking about?" queried Paxton.

"The voting machines have been given an update," said Bascomb.

"Really," sniffed the campaign manager.

"Oh yes. But of course, the update by itself doesn't do us any good. We need a man in the voter registration department to trigger the effect."

"Do tell."

Bascomb hung his head like an embarrassed schoolboy. "I'm sorry to say we have not been able to recruit anyone in Vegas. But there's good news — we have our man in Reno."

Neff folded his arms. "What's this all about?"

Bascomb grinned sheepishly. "I really can't talk about it."

Snell raised a genial hand to forestall Neff's and Paxton's objections. "Gentlemen — Wally knows what he's doing. It's not my money that's going to win this race, it's my intervention."

▼

Outside, the Snell security guard's dog spotted a squirrel foraging for seeds. It gave chase, and the squirrel escaped by running up a tree. Not just any tree — the very tree holding Gaffney's laser microphone and radio transmitter.

Once there, the animal noticed the rubbery insulation on the wires and cables. Like any self-respecting rodent, it went to work chewing through them.

▼

On Lake Tahoe, the radio signal went dead.

"Oh, shit," moaned Gaffney. Those bastards found our stuff."

Solano shared his friend's disappointment, but he was philosophical about it.

"If they don't dust everything for prints and have access to the DMV database, we're okay, I think."

"We hope," said Gaffney nervously, voicing his belief in the worst case scenario.

"Okay, so we don't know their plan. All the same, we learned some things."

"Yeah, what?"

"They're worried. It all hinges on Reno."

"Where they have a spy planted."

"Think what that means — the voting machines won't screw up unless someone tells them to." Solano waggled a finger. "Let's make sure that doesn't happen."

"Oh why not? It's going to be so easy." moaned Gaffney.

36

WILBUR ROLLINS GUYETTE lost his job doing janitor work at the Mini Mart on Liberty Street. The owners were cutting back, they said. Well, fuck them. And, worse, in the past two weeks not a single auto enthusiast had wanted an old car tuned up at his greasy shop on the back road to Sparks. Hey, fuck them too. He made an attempt to apply for unemployment insurance, but the lady at the counter did not have a record of his convenience store employment. Well, fuck her, the sick fucking bureaucrat.

Feeling very sorry for himself, he drove his '59 Cadillac down Virginia Street to the Peppermill Resort just after the dinner hour.

He left his car at the Tires 4 U store, which was closed for the night, shouldered a grimy nylon backpack, and hiked across the wide boulevard to the Peppermill's parking lot. There he sauntered among the cars, looking for items left in view.

He was carrying a stainless steel crescent wrench, partially concealed in a sleeve of his work-stained coveralls. Whenever he spotted a likely bag, case, or box, out came the crescent wrench. A quick jab and side windows became tiny granules of blue-green glass showering down on the asphalt.

Among the victims' vehicles he found a wallet stuffed with credit cards and eighty dollars in cash, a third-generation iPad, a pair of binoculars, a bird book, a nice laptop, a Samsung smartphone, and a fancy Nikon digital camera. He quickly stuffed all the items except an unfortunate bag full of Huggies diapers into his backpack. What the hell, everyone makes mistakes, and overall he was doing very well.

He was helping himself to a ukulele in the back seat of a Ford Mustang when a member of the Peppermill security force noticed him.

"Hey, buddy — stop right there!"

Busted. Guyette dropped his pack and his wrench into the Mustang and stood up.

"Whatcha doing there, pal? You don't look like the owner of that car you're standing at."

Guyette contemplated running, but the security guard had a big black handgun in one hand and a two-way radio in the other. The handgun was pointing at him.

"Got a smasher in the lot, Abe," reported the guard. "Call the dogs for me, will ya?"

Guyette stepped away from the Mustang with his hands up.

"I never took nothing, officer. I was just walking up the street here, when I noticed somebody had been in your lot, smashing people's windows."

"I believe you," said the guard. "Anything you say. Let's just wait until the men in blue arrive, see how they feel."

Guyette stretched his arms out sideways into what he thought of as a crucifixion pose. "Look, I'm kind of down on my luck, need a break. So, yeah, I was looking in the windows, maybe something the smasher left behind, see? Something I could pawn, pay for a meal."

"Down and out, huh? Poor guy. I'm guessing my municipal friends will have a place for you to sleep tonight."

Indeed they did. Five minutes later three City of Reno police vehicles were in the parking lot. One of the officers cuffed Guyette and tossed him into the back seat of his Ford Explorer.

37

CLAIRE FONTAINE, a willowy fifty-year-old public defender, stood by her BMW in the parking lot of the Washoe County Sheriff's Office in north Reno, finishing a cigarette on a crisp morning. Her long and dismal experience with criminals had not eroded her professional optimism, but she was conscious of each day as a psychological strain. She dropped the cigarette butt on the pavement, stamped it out, swept back her graying blonde hair, and marched into the sprawling building, which housed the Washoe County Jail. She was there to see two clients and to bring them each good news.

Julius Aptekar was sitting in an interview room, wearing cuffs chained to a steel table. He was staring gloomily at a complaint sheet detailing his attempted murder of a police officer. He had often imagined the possible consequences of his chosen line of work, and he was resigned to his fate, which he guessed was going to be very bad.

Claire Fontaine stepped into the room. She presented Aptekar with a can of Pepsi, sat down opposite him, and opened her briefcase.

"Now, Mr. Aptekar, it is my duty to inform you of your right to hire any attorney you prefer at any time, and I'll even give you a list of very good ones here in Reno. However, until you do so, I'm still your appointed defender."

"Yeah, that's fine." He opened the Pepsi and drank half of it.

"I have some news," said Fontaine.

"Shoot."

"I have been talking to the prosecutors in this case. How do you feel about pleading to reduced charges?"

Aptekar shrugged listlessly. "Sounds good."

"Here's the deal — the prosecutors will reduce attempted murder to unlawful discharge of a firearm within the Reno city limits. You'll do a year in jail, or maybe two."

"Really. Beats life, I guess. What's stopping them from putting me away for good?"

"As I understand it, the bullet that might have connected your pistol to your victim was smashed flat upon breaking Officer Voss' rib and is of no forensic use. The case is circumstantial. That makes prosecutors nervous."

"The catch . . ?"

"There is one, of course. A big one. In return, you agree to cooperate with the Gaming Control Board and reveal who hired you to shoot Voss."

"Hah. I was never going to shoot Voss. I was supposed to hit that guy Solano."

"We don't need to get into that, Mr. Aptekar. But they will insist on naming names and signing an affidavit. Do you agree?"

Aptekar fell silent. He appeared to study the complaint against him more carefully. He was weighing the consequences of cooperation, wondering if somebody might come after him for telling tales. At length he decided to take his chances.

"Okay, lady, I'm yours."

"Wise decision, Mr. Aptekar."

▼

Waiting in another room nearby was Wilbur Rollins Guyette, the window smasher. Fontaine sat down with him.

"Mr. Guyette? How are you today?"

"Call me Rolly."

"Rolly, then. How are they treating you?"

"The food is terrible."

"Ah, well, of course. This isn't the Atlantis, is it?"

"Don't I wish. You have a candy bar with you, maybe?"

"Sorry, no snacks, but I have something even better. Ready for some good news? Your case is dismissed."

"Unh-huh, not guilty, that's what I told 'em."

"I don't wish to scrutinize the circumstances. The important facts are that the Peppermill has not developed any witness to connect you with car windows you might have smashed, and the police agree that they found no instrument or any stolen goods on your person."

"Right, not me."

"There will be some paperwork, and you're then free to go."

"What about my '59 Caddy?"

"Beg pardon?"

"My car."

Fontaine checked her notes. "It got towed. There was a warning notice in the lot where you parked. You will have to pay the towing company to retrieve it."

"Great. That's what happens to us little guys. Stereotyped. Scape-goated. Abused. And, like always, totally fucked."

"Such language. There's no need for that, Mr. Guyette."

38

JACOB QUARLES, certified public accountant, worked from a fancy office in the El Dorado Hotel building. He was ending his business day by carefully explaining financial complexities to his most important client, Michael Solano, who was staring moodily at the sunset framed in Quarles' fifth-floor window. Because of his recent string of losses, said client would be liable for little more than a nominal estimated tax payment in the current fall quarter.

Solano himself was not convinced. He started to object. Quarles raised a hand.

"Look, Mick — you are allowed to write off gambling losses as business expenses up to the amount you have actually won — earned, really."

"Yeah, I know. Who wrote that law? Somebody bribed somebody, right?"

"Not at all, it's completely normal, and you are the beneficiary."

"I don't want to attract attention. Some of my winnings — and all of my losses — are suspicious."

"Don't tell me, don't explain. There's no such thing as accountant-client privilege."

"For whatever reason, then, the Gaming Control Board is after me. They want blood."

"They won't get it. Your accounts are as clean as the Catholic Church. Well, come to think of what I've been reading, a hell of a lot cleaner. You're clean. Untouchable. Go live."

"Thanks, Jake."

"And if you've got any hot tips — hotter than your recent record anyway — lemme know, okay?"

"I will do that. Don't bet on anything unless you hear from me. You know less about gambling than I do about finance."

"Understood."

They shook hands.

Much relieved, Solano took the elevator to the ground floor and stepped out onto Sierra Street. He turned his baseball cap around backwards, dropped his longboard onto the sidewalk, and pushed off south. He skated along for a block, then swiveled onto the 3rd Street plaza and zigzagged across the wide concrete expanse covering the Union Pacific Railroad tracks.

On West Street he popped an ollie over the curb into a half-empty parking lot, nicely executing a competent kickflip as he did so.

He glided across the lot, gradually slowing down, weaving between the cars. When he reached his Range Rover in the far corner of the lot he pushed the tail of his board onto the asphalt and skidded to a stop.

Jaquoya Cassidy was leaning against the driver's door.

"Hello, Mickey," she said. She was smiling.

"Uh-oh, looks like I'm busted."

"Not necessarily. Can I try?"

"You ride?"

"Oh yeah."

He toed the board toward her. She planted one foot, gave herself a big push with the other, and zipped away toward the plaza, dreads flying. Solano watched her pop over the curb and blast onto the concrete, where she did a huge airborne 180, followed by a quick shove-it, bringing the board back under her feet. She carved around the plaza, then headed back toward the parking lot. She finished up by hopping onto a section of steel rail protecting the automatic payment kiosk and grinding along its length. Finally she rolled back to Solano, who had trouble keeping his jaw from sagging.

"Hands down, girl," he said. "That was pretty good."

She grinned. She was breathing hard.

He cocked his head and regarded her clinically. Regular features. Dark eyes. Attractive in a big-boned kind of way. Her wide smile didn't hurt, and he guessed that her pose, weight on one foot, hip cas-

ually thrust to the side to emphasize her serious curves, indicated flir-
tation. She seemed to have forgotten all about being a cop. He decided
to find out if his guess was a good one.

"Buy you a drink?" he inquired with a negligent wave.

She kicked the longboard up into the air and handed it back. She
was perfectly well aware of the effect she was having on the self-as-
sured gambler.

"In real life, I'd just arrest you on the spot. But here in Reno, in
Nevadaland, how about . . . the Whitewater is just around the corner.
You can use some of your bogus winnings to buy me dinner."

▼

The Whitewater Bistro fronted on the Truckee River, still flowing
impressively in mid-autumn. Solano didn't have a reservation, and
the tables were jammed at happy hour. He signed up with the hostess,
collected glasses of wine at the bar, and led Cassidy along the picturesque walkway above the river's concrete channel, resisting, with con-
siderable difficulty, the impulse to reach for her hand.

They ducked under a lattice bower dripping with late-season wiste-
ria blooms, and sat themselves down on a cozy bench near the Sierra
Street bridge.

"You're never going to arrest me," he said.

"Oh no?" she raised her eyebrows in a pretense of haughty dissent.

"Never. You have no case, and — much more important — you
don't want to."

"Is this — um — is this your *sixth sense* talking?"

"That's right."

"The probability man. Your powers extend beyond the sports
books and slot machines?"

"They do."

She smiled. "So you claim. Well, now, I'm not sure I believe that."

"You don't have to be sure. I am."

He grinned and clicked his glass against hers. She studied him sym-
pathetically, aware of his geeky charm and wary of its allure.

"Aren't you forgetting my wounded colleague?"

"Officer Voss?"

"After he recovers from the bullet meant for you, he's likely to insist on an indictment."

"You'll wave him off."

"Oh I will, will I?"

"I think you're very persuasive," said Solano, eyeing a text message that was flashing on his mobile phone: their table was ready.

▼

Over steaks, arugula salads, and large glasses of red wine, criminal and cop worked to get comfortable with each other by the light of a flickering candle.

"Who's your lawyer, Mickey? You're going to need one, whether you sense it or not."

Solano nodded cheerfully. "I'm well equipped. The best in town."

"May I ask the name?"

"Cameron Hayes. He's like a father to me."

Cassidy grimaced. "Be careful there. In the room, when we gossip, we think he's mobbed up."

"Didn't you listen to me? Forget your *go directly to jail* crap, okay? We're having dinner."

"Just saying."

"O-ho! I'm guessing Hayes beat you guys like a drum on a case or two."

Cassidy pursed her lips. "You could say that."

Solano gazed at her over the candle flame. Her eyes were warm and wide, contradicting her knitted brows. He sensed room to lobby his agenda.

"All right, Madam Justice, here's something important to talk about. Election fraud. It's happening. The Paxton campaign has paid some guy in the Washoe County Registrar of Voters — some inspector — to activate the sabotage code in Patriotic's voting machines."

"There you go again. Like I may have mentioned, my office is not into politics."

"Me neither." He searched her face for some sign of interest, some spark, but saw only professional skepticism. "On the other hand, I kind of like democracy. Especially when practiced on the up-and-up."

She gave him an ironic grin. "On the up-and-up — like you."

"Geez, you are tough. My friend Gaffney and I got surveillance records of the deal. I'll hand them to you."

Cassidy was disturbed by Solano's assertion. "Surveillance? You? You're kidding, right?"

"Paxton was taking a campaign break at Lloyd Snell's house, up the hill at Northstar. We were in the woods with a laser mike. That thing — hah! — it actually worked, at least for a while."

"You really did this?"

"Yeah, we did." He reached into his shirt pocket for a small audio device and brandished it playfully in front of Cassidy's nose. "Got the man on my voice recorder."

"Without a court order or probable cause?"

"Does it matter? We were never actually on his property. Got those bastards plotting to steal a senate seat. Wake up already."

A few minutes earlier Cassidy was gazing into her dinner companion's soft brown eyes contemplating romance. Now she was all business.

"Listen, Mickey. What you did would be ruled inadmissible in court. What you're telling me is a good story, okay? But no cop I ever met would take action based on your" — she wagged a finger — "boy scout hike. You understand? Democracy, the law, it's tricky."

Solano sat back, stung by her dismissal. "Boy scout? Ouch, that hurts. But I'm not giving up on this. Come on, you can help."

"Here's how I can help. Going to court won't work. But maybe you can scare up some adverse publicity with your recorded voices. Talk to KNVR again, they love this kind of stuff."

"I dunno. They're like . . . see no evil unless they see it on both sides, know what I mean? Cowards."

Cassidy leaned forward and patted Solano's hand. "If you believe, keep trying. Only don't lean on me."

She stood up to go.

"I'm not supposed to blab, but — *ahhhh* — what the hell." She blew out a big sigh. "We arrested your hitter."

Solano was thunderstruck. "Now *that* is some piece of news."

"Lucky break — miraculous really. Suspect is a pro from back east named Julius Aptekar. He's pleading to reduced charges, and guess what? In return he gave us Worden and Barber, who hired him."

Solano swallowed. He sucked in some air. "So that's why you showed up in the parking lot."

"Unh-huh. The Silverlode will be restructuring with new management pretty soon. And like you predicted, you're off the hook. For now, anyway."

"Thanks for the heads-up."

"Don't mention it. I mean — Do. Not. Mention. It. To anyone."

"Cross my heart."

"You can relax. You don't need Silverlode's involvement in some imaginary voter fraud to wiggle out of trouble anymore."

"Ouch again. You think that's why I'm all over Paxton?" He leaned forward. He was angry. "True, that's how it started. But his plans are not imaginary, and I'm not fooling around."

Cassidy flicked her dreads and made a little finger wave.

"Dessert another time, what do you say?"

Before Solano could say anything, she was striding away between the tables and out the door.

39

CASSIDY WAS NURSING A HEADACHE. A hangover, really. A professional one. She was almost certain that Solano was in on the Silverlode's illegal activities, and yet he did not seem to be the kind of criminal she was familiar with after ten years of police work. At least that's what she was telling herself, and she knew she was taking sides, knew that Solano's boyish charm was clouding her judgment.

She strode through the Gaming Control Board's Reno offices in search of Luke Voss. The receptionist had mentioned that the heroic officer was back on the job this morning, having recovered from the shot that smashed a rib and punctured a lung.

She found him at the cubicle he favored. He was stuffing papers and memories into filing boxes.

"Luke. You're back. Good to see you," she said.

Voss looked up from his labors.

"Jaquoya. Watch this" — he raised both arms over his head — "first time I can do that since the big bang."

She nodded approval. "You are totally buff, officer."

"Feel like a human being again, anyway."

Cassidy leaned up against his cubby wall. "As you know, the Silverlode case is jelling. Those guys are going down."

Voss stood up straight. He leaned back to take a good look at his sometime partner. "Indeedy-deed. Thanks to you."

She nodded to accept the mild compliment. Voss paused to evaluate her presence in his workspace. "You didn't stop by to cheer me up, you're here to wonder about the hitter's target — what's his name? — Solano?"

"I guess I am."

"Ahhh," he chuckled. "You're sweet on the guy. I'm jealous."

"Hey, hey, hey — two years ago, for five minutes, we were an item.

Now you're a married man. You owe me benefit-of-the-doubt on this."

"Mmm, prickly this morning."

"So, what do we do?"

"Well, the Silverlode boys sure thought he was a threat to their schemes. Bring him in, turn on the heat."

"We're going to nail Barber and Worden anyway. What's the point?"

"The point? Jesus, Jaquoya, *he's a crook.*"

Cassidy compressed her lips to resist the idea. "Maybe, maybe not. He's got a high-powered lawyer. Going to be tough to convict."

Voss picked up a pair of reading glasses and put them on. He stared at her through them.

"You . . . a cop in love . . . with a fucking crook."

"I did not confess to any such thing," insisted Cassidy. "However" — she raised a finger to rebut the critique and reassure herself — "I think he has redeeming qualities."

"Oh boy."

Voss shook his head. He was amused by her hopelessly impaired judgment. "Normally, sweetheart, I would overrule you on this and put the grab on him. State's witness if nothing else. At the worst, witness protection."

He removed his glasses and dropped them into one of the filing boxes on his desk.

"See these boxes?"

At last she noticed them. "Yeah . . ?"

"The truth is, you can do whatever you want with Solano. I'm out of here."

Cassidy gawked stupidly at the man and his boxes, suddenly aware of a big change coming.

"Where to?"

"*Blackball, Inc.* Security company. Offices in Lost Wages."

"You can't be quitting, you love the life."

"I found out how to temper my affection."

"Well, shit."

Voss hoisted a box and took a step toward the exit. He grimaced under the weight. "Solano? I give up. Maybe you'll be a good influence."

Cassidy leaned forward and kissed him lightly on the cheek.

"Thanks for the vote of confidence."

He made a face.

"Don't get shot, babe. It hurts."

40

SOLANO WAS INSTALLED in his home office in the hills above the western flank of Reno. He had been there for hours, digging through Osgood's partially deciphered computer code, when he stumbled on lines that were almost readable . . .

```
<< :blk7: {put (text:&quot; PRINT DEMONSTRATION
BALLOT &quot:endtext) into displaybuff;} put (dis-
playbuff) into screen_top; ontouch >>> {callback
<< :blk7: if (call==go) {<< :blk9: write hot
alert::#55;}} rtn;
```

. . . almost, but not quite. He was looking at a user interface command, for sure, but he wondered what it triggered. He entered the search term *hot alert* into his text editor, pressed return, and was rewarded with another chunk of mysterious code:

```
hot alert::#55=text:&quot; MACHINE MALFUNCTION
CALL TECH SUPPORT &quot:endtext; >>> {set cycle.
infinite = T; << :blk9: >> doomsday();}
```

He stood up and stared out his picture window at the city below and the eastern mountains beyond. Planes were taking off and landing at the airport. Cars were rolling along the highways and thoroughfares. Steam was rising from the city's thermal power plant, and the morning sun was shining benignly on the tranquil scene. A normal fall day in Reno. He took a deep breath and let the air slowly escape. All was anything but normal.

"Damn. It's so simple."

What began as a suspicion that grew into an embarrassing obsession was now revealed as a fact. A little chill rippled up his spine. He thought he knew how Patriotic's compromised voting machines would tilt the election, what Frank Osgood's code was intended to do.

He was guessing, of course, but he had no doubts.

He called Cassidy.

"Morning, officer. I know you don't care, but I just figured out how Paxton's campaign is going to sabotage our voting machines."

"You're right, Mickey — I don't care. Not about the election. But you? I'm worried. Stop scratching your conspiracy itch, okay?"

"Not okay!"

He hung up and called his lawyer.

"Yo, Mick," greeted Hayes brightly. The man was in a jovial mood. "Hear about the Silverlode brass?"

"Yeah, I heard."

"Great news. Hah, this is funny — Barber called, wants me to represent him."

"No, no, no, that is *so wrong.*"

"Every man deserves his day in court, Mickey."

"Good God, Cam. Where are your morals?"

"I don't have any. Just an accurate sense of professional ethics."

"Forget your fees for a moment. I figured out how Paxton's crew is going to try and tip the election."

"That again, still on the fraud train."

"They've got a guy in the Registrar's office. They're going to screw up voting machines all over the city."

"They are? Don't bet the rent money, kiddo."

"Remember my sixth sense, Cam? It's what pays your retainer. And it's telling me this bet's a winner."

Hayes was not sold.

"I'll pass the word, but I think this is just your paranoia talking. Jesus, Mickey, have a nice day."

Solano didn't have a working phone number for Gaffney, and it annoyed him. He swore inwardly over the man's furtive habits, trudged outside, fired up his Range Rover, and drove slowly into town in a sour mood.

▼

First stop was at the KNVR studio. He parked on the street and marched into the reception area. His mood did not improve inside, because the walls were covered with photo murals of the station's past and present stars, and on the wall behind the middle-aged woman guarding the front desk was a huge portrait of the glamorous Gigi Newhouse.

"Excuse me," began Solano. "I have some important information about the election next month."

"Yes? What sort of information?"

"It's going to be rigged, and everyone needs to know about it."

The receptionist blanched. Her finger hovered over a hidden *Summon Security* button. But then, looking closely at her informant, who was smiling a weary smile, she decided that he wasn't actually deranged.

"I remember you" — she gestured toward the mural behind her desk — "Miss Newhouse's friend, right? Try our tip line, sir. Staff will be very interested, I'm sure."

She indicated the house phone on a table across the room. Solano grunted, strolled over, and picked it up.

"KNVR Tip Line," recited a bored male voice. "Here at the Pulsing Heart Of The News In Reno, We Heart Information. What have you got for us?"

Solano stared at the ceiling. "I have knowledge that the coming senate election will be rigged in favor of that guy Paxton."

"Beg pardon?"

"Paxton's campaign is tampering with our voting machines."

"Unh-huh. That sounds bad. Also improbable. Do you have, like, any evidence to buttress your claim?"

"Yes, I do. Two different things. First, I have deciphered the recent Patriotic Decision Systems' voting machine code and discovered sabotage."

"Code? What are we talking about?"

"The voting machines run on computer code. I decoded it."

"Really."

"Yes, really. I'm a programmer. And, more important, I guess — I overheard members of Paxton's team tell the man himself how they have paid a voting inspector to alter the machines' behavior."

"Behavior?"

"How they tally the votes." Solano heard, in the Tip Line's ensuing silence, grave doubt. "I have a flash drive with a recording."

"Hmm. That's something. Leave it with the receptionist. We'll have a listen. Do you want to be known or interviewed if we run a story?"

"No thanks."

"Anonymous. That's okay, that's what the Tip Line is for."

Solano grumpily handed a tiny USB flash drive to the receptionist and headed for his car. He wouldn't allow himself to hope for results.

▼

The campaign to return Maynard Ives to the U.S. Senate for a fourth term was headquartered in Las Vegas, but it maintained a branch office in Reno, in the El Dorado Hotel building, a floor below Solano's accountant.

Solano introduced himself to the volunteer behind the desk. She was stapling a pile of small *I'm For Ives* signs to flimsy wooden stakes. She looked to be twenty-something, barely old enough to order a beer in a bar. Her youth made him wonder about the effectiveness of Ives' aides and associates. He reeled off his worries about the impending election without much enthusiasm.

The volunteer called into a back room and a senior staff member appeared. The man was in his fifties, awkwardly dressed in a rumpled suit. Solano thought he seemed flustered and distracted, probably by the difficulties of running an undermanned operation.

"Election fraud? How would that happen?" wondered the staffer.

"Paxton's campaign is going to sabotage our voting machines," announced Solano.

The staffer took a backward step, clearly worried about Solano's sanity. "Who are you? What kind of ants got into *your* pants?"

Solano winced. He offered a sardonic smile. "I'm a former coder. I've seen the source of Patriotic's software."

"Patriotic? Who's that?"

Solano was amazed. The staffer didn't know who manufactured Nevada's voting equipment, apparently. "Patriotic makes our voting machines."

"Oh, right."

"They're computers. They run code. That's how they work."

"Of course. Got it."

Solano moved on to the next bit of damnation. "Better yet, I overheard people on the Paxton team talk about bribing someone from the Registrar's office."

"You don't say? That would be a scandal. But the senator is up in the polls today, and we see citizens reacting positively to our message. Now, I don't know a thing about computer code, but I believe Nevada voting machines have to leave a paper trail. Is that right?"

"True, it's the law."

"So . . . I don't think there's much to worry about."

Solano shook his head. This guy, what a dunce.

"A paper trail will only mean anything in a recount. You'll have to file a lawsuit. Years will go by while Paxton takes his seat in Washington."

The staffer manufactured a genial smile. He patted Solano on the arm.

"We'll take our chances."

▼

Solano decided to confront Patriotic Decision Systems directly. He drove across town to their headquarters in the industrial park east of the Reno airport.

"What exactly are you accusing us of, Mr. Solano?" inquired the Patriotic executive, a fellow in a short-sleeved shirt and tie named Joel

Toravian. The son of the company founder was called to deal with that crazy man in the lobby by a junior manager anxious to dodge all responsibility. Solano thought Toravian looked like one of those NASA dudes who once ran the moon missions.

"Frank Osgood wrote the update code for your voting machines, right?" asked Solano.

"Frank worked for us, yes, yes. Tragic loss. I can't really discuss his tasks or activities."

"Understood. But here's the thing — I have seen his source code, and it contains commands that will sabotage the operation of your machines."

Toravian regarded Solano coolly. He wasn't shy about letting some hostility show. "First of all, Frank's code is proprietary. How on Earth did you ever get hold of it — if you actually did?"

"I can't tell you."

Toravian's brow furrowed. Then he laughed bitterly. He jabbed a finger at Solano. "Wait a minute. Oh, for God's sake, it's obvious — that maniac Gaffney. Gaffney, right?"

Solano was prepared to lie and didn't blink. "I don't know anyone named Gaffney," he replied.

"Lucky you." Toravian passed a hand across his jaw, reliving unpleasant memories. "We had to fire him. What a nutball."

"So? Fired? The facts remain . . ."

"Impossible. Our code is written in a military language. It's fully obfuscated. If you saw it, you could never understand it, even if you're an accomplished coder" — he glared at Solano — "which I doubt."

"Computer science degree, five years at HighScore, down in the nuts and bolts department," stated Solano, offering his credentials with a shrug. "Trust me on this."

Toravian sniffed dismissively. "And the idea itself — sabotage? — that is *ridiculous.* You're impugning Patriotic's reputation and honesty with this nonsense. You damn well better destroy any material of ours, however you got it, or you will face charges of revealing our trade secrets. That will be expensive."

"I'm not worried, Mr. Toravian," said Solano, turning to leave. "But you should be."

▼

Three pitches, three strikes.

Solano considered the situation, then marshaled his wits, his will, and his optimism, got out his smartphone, and used it to pinpoint the location of the Washoe County Registrar of Voters office in the County Administration Building, a few blocks north of I-80.

After preliminary explanations at the front desk, a severely dressed older woman arrived from the labyrinth of back offices to hear his worries and complaints.

"You're sure about this, Mr. — who?"

"Solano. And yes, I'm pretty sure. At least, if you have installed Patriotic's recent firmware update."

"We have."

"Then, watch out. I have knowledge — a recording — that claims the Paxton campaign has bribed one of your inspectors to do damage come election day."

She appraised the young man facing her. From her matronly point of view he looked like an eager teenager, but that actually solidified his complaint, since she assumed all computer experts were children.

"Show me," she said, and started away down the hall with a come-along gesture.

Solano followed the woman to a back room where a number of spare voting machines were standing by. The woman plugged one of them in and started it up.

"Here we are," she said.

"Patriotic's Ridge E-29," noted Solano. "I've been reading up on these things. Administrators can insert an ID card and mess with the settings, right?"

"We don't *mess* with anything around here, Mr. Solano. An inspector or the managers of a polling place can request test ballots, print test backups, verify data integrity, and lock everything up once the polls are closed. But that's all."

Solano nodded. "What I've learned is that hacked machines will show the command, *Print Demonstration Ballot* instead of *Print Test Ballot*. Running that command will put them out of action."

"Oh?"

"That will disappoint a lot of would-be voters, right?"

"I should say so!" said the woman, raising her hands in alarm and dismay. "Let's see now, I have an admin card . . ."

She lifted a credit-card-sized slab of plastic from a pocket on her suit. "If I plug this in, I'll see the offending command?"

"That's the idea. Yup. Let's try it, get to the bottom of this."

The woman donned a pair of glasses and inserted her card into the Ridge E-29 reader. The splash screen graphics gave way to a text menu:

```
VERIFY DATA
LOCK DATA CARTRIDGE
PRINT TEST RECEIPT
PRINT TEST BALLOT
```

"Oh dear. I don't see the command you mentioned, do you?" She eyeballed her visitor accusingly over the rims of her glasses.

Solano backed away from the machine. He was stumped, puzzled, and embarrassed.

"Oh shit," he said. "Whoops, pardon my French."

"No need. I'm delighted to know that our upcoming election will go smoothly after all. Thanks for proving it."

Solano's invisible tail was curling between his legs, but he still had hopes. "Damn — is it possible that some cards have special codes?"

"None that I'm aware of."

Solano nodded miserably.

"You said one of our inspectors had been bribed," reminded the woman. "Name?"

"Sorry, I didn't get a name, I don't have anyone's name for you."

The woman slowly shook her head. Her long face registered the kind of pity reserved for the lame and the halt.

"Goodbye, Mr. Solano."

▼

In the studios of KNVR-TV, Maggie Morrison and Diego Ramirez were listening to Solano's recording of the Paxton conspiracy on a little laptop computer:

> . . . *I'm sorry to say we have not been able to re-zakk any-*
> *one in Vegas. But zorozz — we have our man in Reno.*

Strange whistling noises interrupted the speaker. Then the recording briefly cleared up for a moment:

> *I really can't talk about it.*

More squeals and pops, then:

> *Gentlemen — Warrip knows what he's doing. It's not my*
> *money that's going to win this race, it's my interzazz. . . .*

Morrison and Ramirez replayed the recording several times.

"Not very good quality, is it?"

"Total crap — like all those surveillance videos people send us."

"Who's *Warrip?*"

"Thought I heard *Wally,* but I'd never testify under oath."

"And someone thinks his *interzazz* will win the race. Someone with money, apparently."

"Think it's real?"

"Probably."

"Want to run with it?"

"On the air? Are you out of your mind?"

NOVEMBER

41

NEWS of the day.

At KNVR-TV, Maggie Morrison and Diego Ramirez were giddy with excitement, because their lead story didn't involve fires or car crashes; snow was falling in the Sierra. First storm of the season, and the news anchors were settling a bet.

"Diego, you doubled down on a late start, November fifteenth, if I remember correctly," said Morrison.

Ramirez hung his head in a theatrical display of loser shame. "I did, Mags, I did and no denying it. You bet October thirty-first. You win."

"Remind me *what* I'm winning."

"Fifty silver dollars to feed the slots at a casino of your choice."

"Third year in a row, Diego," teased Morrison.

"Don't rub it in," sighed her partner.

"So what's the story? How much of the white stuff? Will Reno see snowflakes tonight?" They both turned to the KNVR weatherman, who joined his colleagues in front of the camera. The backdrop dissolved into night views of the Mount Rose ski resort, where grooming machines were grinding up and down slopes illuminated by furiously bright LED lights. The images were blurred by a thick veil of falling snow.

"What you're looking at, folks, is — yup, live — the real thing," confirmed the meteorologist, "and it's a blizzard."

"Oh no," gasped Morrison. "Will I need chains tomorrow morning?"

"Not to worry, Maggie. Some neighborhoods around town may see a flake or two drifting down, but the real action is confined to the high country. Look for plows on the road, but I-80 will still get you to Truckee with minimum delay."

"Hear that everyone? Good news for a change."

After a commercial break, Ramirez took note of political developments.

"We're on the eve of the election, boys and girls and eligible voters. If you're like us, you can't wait for election day — after that, the shouting, the name-calling, the slurs, and the scandals will fade into history."

He shook his head in mock lament.

"Then we can focus on more interesting topics — like the Oakland Raiders, undefeated so far this year. Preparing for their Vegas debut, right, Mags?"

Morrison gave her co-anchor and their audience a peevish nod.

"Looks like the scandals you mentioned are getting bigger, not smaller, Diego. Today we learned of a management shuffle at the Silverlode Casino. Edward Barber, the general manager, is out, along with Richard Worden, his deputy, and — isn't this interesting? — Jennifer Penrose, his security manager. Does that last name ring a bell? She was the woman accusing the senator of sexual harassment. The moves seem to confirm rumors about that company's involvement in attacks on Senator Ives' moral character, attacks that may be traceable to his opponent's campaign."

"I'm sure we'll find out all about it — in three or four years," griped Ramirez. "Meanwhile, with only a few days left, the race is tight. Ives holds a slender lead, but it's going to go down to the wire, and *voter turnout* will decide the outcome." He grinned. "Either that or, heh-heh — *voter turnoff* — take your pick."

42

ON THE FIRST MONDAY in November, election eve, assigned poll workers assembled at the Gilbert Wheaton Middle School in Reno Ward 3 to prepare for their big day.

Osman Daiyari, the polling place manager, picked up the necessary voting equipment at the Registrar of Voters Office just before it closed at 3:00 PM and drove it to the school in his Ford Econoline van. There he was joined by Patricia Galbraith, the assistant manager, Joseph Boyd, the intake specialist, and Anne Weiss, the roster specialist, around an hour later.

Kids were still streaming in and out of the doors, reveling in after-school sports and pranks when the team unloaded the voting machines and their associated materials from Daiyari's truck. Stepping around the boisterous youths, they carried everything into the school's main assembly hall, which had been cordoned off for their use.

Daiyari came to the United States from the Hashemite Kingdom of Jordan. He was proud of his hard-won citizenship and proud to volunteer on behalf of democracy. His co-workers regarded him fondly as a good-natured perfectionist and weren't the least bit surprised or annoyed when he pulled a checklist out of the accordion file and insisted on reading through it twice.

By early evening everything was ready: voter lists, voter cards, brochures, forms, signs, ten voter card activators, and ten Patriotic Ridge E-29 voting machines erected on spindly legs and separated by privacy screens.

Daiyari and Galbraith checked the machine's serial numbers, recorded them on the Manager's Verification Statement, plugged them in, turned them on, and printed test pages in accordance with pre-election protocols. Everything worked. The team turned the machines off, locked the place up and took the keys home.

▼

At 5:45 AM next morning, Tuesday, election day itself, the team was back at the Wheaton School ready to oversee the big event. Daiyari brought tall espresso drinks. Galbraith brought bear claws and sticky buns. After pinning on their badges and ceremonially signing the Oath of Office Sheet, the team wasted no time drinking coffee and scarfing down pastries, fortifying themselves for the possibility of a trying day.

"Heavy turnout, or not?" queried Weiss. "What do we think?"

Galbraith and Boyd just shook their heads. Daiyari was of the same mind. "Americans are lazy," he said. "Not many will bother to come."

"I think we'll be swamped," returned Weiss. She was excited. "Ives versus Paxton? This is big."

"Any bets?" wondered Galbraith.

"Even in Nevada, public servants of democracy should not gamble," Daiyari warned.

"Okay, no money. Scones and doughnuts then," said Weiss.

"No need to bet. Today, we will see with our eyes how it all works. I am hopeful," said Daiyari, in a tone that failed to convey any sense of actual hope.

"Come on, Oz. It's always a mess," said Boyd cheerfully. "That's us, your fellow American citizens."

Daiyari and Galbraith re-checked the voting machines and confirmed that the serial numbers matched what they had written on the Manager's Verification Statement. Then Daiyari used a pair of scissors to cut the violet seals on each *open/closed* switch cover, flipped the switches inside to *open,* and re-sealed the covers. The machines were now configured to record votes. Zero Proof Reports automatically rolled out of the Voter Verified Paper Audit Trail printers attached to each machine.

To complete their preparations, Daiyari fetched the Distance Marker String from the team's polling place kit. He gave one end to

Galbraith and marched out through the school entrance. He walked until he felt the string snap taut. There he dropped an orange traffic cone on the sidewalk and fixed a warning sign to the top:

NO ELECTIONEERING
WITHIN 100 FEET OF POLLING PLACES

A few minutes before the polls were to open at 7:00 AM, the team had a visitor from the Registrar of Voters Office. He was a large man in his mid-fifties with graying hair and scraggly beard. A wrinkled sports jacket concealed a modest paunch.

"Hi, there, people," he said, showing off a plastic ID card. "I'm here to double-check your setup."

Galbraith's nose twitched. The odor of tobacco smoke issued from the man's clothing. Daiyari examined his ID. The ROV logo was authentic. Under the title *Administrator*, the nicely printed name read, *TOM FLYNN.*

"Mr. Flynn. We've never had anyone double-check us before. Why now?"

"It's a random spot-check deal. See that everything's okay."

Daiyari frowned. "We are very okay."

Flynn moved to the voting machines. He waved a doubtful hand at the lineup.

"These damn things — there's a lot to go wrong, they're not as reliable as I'd like. So, we're checking, anticipating trouble, just in case."

He inserted his ID — it looked just like a voter card — into the first machine's activation slot. The touch screen displayed a menu. Flynn pressed a finger on one of the commands, the very one that worried Solano:

PRINT DEMONSTRATION BALLOT

The VVPAT printer spewed out a test ballot. Flynn repeated the procedure on six of the remaining machines. He grinned satisfaction.

"Everything looks good here. You're good to go."

▼

The first voter didn't show up until almost 8:30 AM, but after that, Reno residents were lined up out the door and onto the sidewalk. For a short while everything ran smoothly, but then, after recording a few votes, all seven Ridge E-29 machines 'spot-checked' by Flynn failed. They all displayed the same dire message:

```
MACHINE MALFUNCTION CALL TECH SUPPORT
```

So they did. Galbraith was on the horn to the ROV for ten minutes before anyone picked up. Then she learned that machines were failing all over town. Service technicians were stretched thin, but someone would be at the Wheaton School to troubleshoot *as soon as possible.*

Meanwhile, three of the machines were still working. A few voters were able to cast ballots, and the audit trail printers proved that they did so by cranking out Nevada's required paper backups. But the line grew long, and people stuck in the line grew angry. Daiyari walked back and forth among the frustrated citizens, trying to reassure them. Nevertheless, after half an hour the line began to shorten as potential voters tired of waiting and drifted away. Soon there was no line at all.

As promised, a technician — not Flynn — eventually arrived to repair and reset the machines. But try as he might, he couldn't restore them to operational status.

43

AT 10:00 AM, Solano was back from a long suburban run whose superstitious purpose was to clear his mind of any black thoughts that might magically warp the election outcome. He was sitting in his Reno office, still in his jogging gear, glued to five TV sets, all of them broadcasting stories about election progress. Ives was ahead in Las Vegas, showing his appeal in the big city, as expected.

"I'm very confident," the senator announced.

On the other hand . . .

"We're winning, folks. Nevada wants change, and we are going to give it to them," vowed Paxton.

The candidates waved enthusiastically to their respective supporters and to the cameras circling them like vultures.

Solano was simultaneously sweaty, sleepy, bored, and restless. Many hours stretched ahead until the polls closed, and who knew what was happening?

His mood changed when one of KNVR's news anchors — that guy Ramirez — reported voting machine failures at a few polling places. He sat up straight when the other Reno channels picked up the same story.

"Uh-oh."

His attention was interrupted by his doorbell ringing and fists pounding on his door. He switched the source of one of his screens to closed-circuit TV. Bill Gaffney was standing on his porch.

"Trixie, front door . . ."

"Have you heard?" growled his friend as he rushed inside. "You getting this? The Paxton plan is going down."

Solano raised his eyebrows. "KNVR says there are just a few failures. Could be Patriotic's shoddy machinery."

"No way, bro. Patriotic *hardware* is bulletproof. Listen to the radio — voting machines are conking out all over the city."

Solano commanded his audiobot to tune in the local PBS radio station, where he heard the Washoe County Registrar of Voters wringing her hands over a thirty percent failure rate, unheard of in any previous contest.

"Shit. You're right, this is trouble."

"I made a list," said Gaffney, waving a sheet of paper. "Earlier, the voter babe mentioned which precincts are getting hit. Wanna guess?"

"The Ives precincts."

"You know it, pal. And down in Vegas, networks are making predictions — without a big turnout, Paxton is going to win."

Solano hung his head. "I tried to warn them. Tried everything."

Gaffney marched back and forth. "I will not tolerate a rigged election. Plan B, Mickey, Plan B."

Gaffney sounded fierce. He sounded determined. Solano was alarmed.

"That doesn't sound good, Bill. Better tell me."

"Oh no, that might alert the spies."

"Those wacky spies. Think I'll spill the beans?"

"You never know. I'm gonna act. Solo operation. Take responsibility."

Before Solano could insist on an explanation, his doorbell rang again. He eyed the closed circuit TV feed. Now Jaquoya Cassidy was tapping her foot on the doormat. Solano was temporarily elated by her unexpected arrival. A vision of future possibilities that stretched beyond election day flitted through his agitated mind. Surely, the sexy Gaming Control Board cop was not here to arrest him.

"Trixie . . ?"

In came Cassidy, looking upbeat. She was wearing a down jacket over her usual tight jeans. She had a bottle of champagne in her hand.

"Hi, Mickey. Today's the day." She hefted the champagne. "Got some glasses? I'll make mimosas."

Gaffney stared at the newcomer. "Who's your friend?" he asked.

"Jaquoya, Bill — Bill, Jaquoya. Watch out, she's a cop."

"Off duty today," said Cassidy, shaking Gaffney's hand. "Well, Mr. Conspiracy Theory, you were worried about fraud, but it looks like Ives will pull out the victory."

Solano and Gaffney glanced at each other. "When did you hear this?"

"About an hour ago. Exit polls in Vegas give him a big lead."

Solano scratched his head. "Important update — voting machines are breaking down all over Reno. If they don't get fixed, and pronto, Paxton will squeak through."

"What?"

"This is fraud. And the sabotage code is working its magic," insisted Gaffney.

Cassidy was hard to convince. "How can you be sure?"

Solano sighed, turned on his laptop, and brought up the code he had worked so hard to decipher. He pointed to the command that sent the machines into a tizzy for Cassidy's enlightenment.

"Paxton's boys have bribed some official-type guy. When the crook executes the command you see here, it's over. The machines then fail," explained Gaffney.

"Except," groaned Solano, "I didn't see the command at all on the test machines at the Registrar of Voters."

Gaffney thought about the problem. "The guy they bribed must have a special card. That's it. Gotta be. The command is tied to the number on his ID."

Cassidy stared at the code on display. "This looks like monkeys trying to write Shakespeare."

"Whatever works. Ives is hosed, and so are we."

Cassidy wasn't so pessimistic. "If you were a criminal doing bad things that left evidence lying around, wouldn't you want a way to cover your tracks?"

"How could he do that?"

"You know, reverse your sabotage after the damage is done."

To Cassidy, schooled in law enforcement, it was obvious. To the comparatively naïve coder geeks, it was a head-slapper.

"Holy shit," said Gaffney. "We've got to find the command that breaks the failure loop."

Solano looked at the link between the command to print a demonstration ballot and the sabotage code:

```
{set cycle.infinite = T; << :blk9: >> doomsday();}
```

He searched for the *doomsday()* function, but it didn't turn up right away.

"Damn, the loop it calls isn't in this file," he muttered.

Another search, longer than the last one. Finally, there it was, hiding inexplicably within the *manageupdate.red* file:

```
doomsday() {if (cycle.infinite == T) {<< :blk9:
doloop();} else if (cycle.infinite == F) {exit >>
:blk6: >>;}}
```

"Crap in a hat. We've got a global state boolean!"

"My God. The controller."

Both men felt like they had just trapped an exotic animal hitherto unknown to science. Nobel prize here we come. But their problems were not yet solved.

"So . . . who *resets* the state of *cycle-dot-fucking-infinite???*"

Another search, longer still.

"Forget the mimosas. Any coffee around here?" wondered Cassidy.

Solano pointed toward his kitchen without looking up. "Coffee, donuts, thataway."

The mystified cop left the coders to their search terms. They tried a dozen without success before she strolled back into the office with hot coffee and a half-eaten maple bar.

"Still at it," she noted, arching an eyebrow and twirling a dreadlock. "In the movies, it only takes five minutes."

Solano was grim. "Yeah, in the movies. This is I-R-L."

It took them two hours.

"Hey, Bill, I thought you stole everything."

"That's right, I did."

Solano was frustrated to the breaking point. "Something's missing. I can't find a command to reset our state var anywhere."

Gaffney sat down cross-legged on the floor to think things over.

"You know what? I told Frank he was going to get in big trouble, get his ass fired, and he just smiled. He said he'd taken a hostage."

Solano perked up. A glimmer of light was poking through the far end of their search tunnel. "You think he kidnapped one of the files, hid it somewhere as a bargaining chip. Is that it?"

Gaffney jumped up and paced the room. *"Kidnapped,* you just said. Of course! The hostage is one of his files, a vital one, squirreled away. But where?"

Solano stared at his computer screen. A thought bubbled up. "You kidnap somebody, that means you want money. Osgood was looking for a big raise, right?"

"Yeah, that cocky little shit."

"How does a kidnapper make demands, huh? How?"

Gaffney's face lit up. "Ransom note!"

Solano grinned. "Exactamundo, dude! And where does his note go, if he wants to send — or better yet — hide it?"

"Email system, it's beyond huge. We gotta hack Patriotic's server."

Solano's mood darkened again. "Except — tiny hitch — we don't have the dead guy's network password, even if it still worked."

Gaffney clapped his hands together. "No, Osgood was careful, but we can get in via the boss." He chuckled sardonically. "Hah — that Toravian kid, daddy's little genius — derp! His password is the license plate on his Beamer."

Solano stood up from his chair and beckoned Gaffney to take his place. "You're up, then. Have at it."

Gaffney addressed the Patriotic network and typed a password:

EVOTER1

It worked. Five minutes later he was scanning through the digital tonnage of Patriotic Decision Systems' email accounts, the rambling work of dozens of employees over dozens of years. Thousands upon thousands of messages.

"We just fell down the fucking rabbit hole," complained Gaffney impatiently.

"So we do like Alice, take a pill — big one first. Search for anything *dot-red,*" ordered Solano.

Gaffney did so. Solano's laptop churned heroically. Even so, running at three-point-three gigahertz, the machine's quad-core central processor was laboring. Several minutes went by in silence, culminating in the dismal notice, *word not found.* The would-be hackers' spirits sagged.

"Nothing there, bro."

But Solano wasn't ready to give up. "Now try the small pill — do a negative search, anything *NOT dot-pst*, those damn email texts."

Gaffney initiated another long search grind. But this time, after several more minutes of excruciating suspense, the machine turned up something called *slipstream.chk.*

"Well well well. Look at that."

He copied the file to his host's laptop.

Now Solano took over. He changed the file suffix to *dot-red* and entered the search term, *cycle.infinite.*

"Cross your fingers, Bill."

He pressed the enter key, and following another nerve-racking interval, their target unceremoniously revealed itself:

```
hot alert::#66=text:&quot CLEAR VVPAT PAPER JAM
&quot:endtext; ontouch >>> {<< :blk9: && :blk7:
>> reset cycle.infinite = F;}
```

"Hey, hey, hey!" whooped Solano. The two code hunters stood up straight, slapped high fives, bumped fists.

Cassidy tore herself away from KNVR's ongoing election coverage.

"You found it."

"Damn right we did, hey, bro?"

High fives again, this time behind their backs with turnaround spins.

"The question," she posed, restraining any excitement of her own, "is — what are we going to do about it? Did you vote already?"

Gaffney laughed self-consciously. "Can't vote. Not registered. Gotta keep a low profile."

Cassidy rolled her eyes. "Some politico you are. Mickey? How about it?"

"Not yet. And you, the model citizen?"

She nodded a vigorous affirmative. "Early this morning." She squinted at the code. *"equal-sign-F* means *false*, right? Is that what I'm seeing?"

"Yup. That is correct, ha-ha."

"If we reset the global-whatsis to *false* on all the machines, they'll go back to work, yes?"

Gaffney and Solano both felt their goofy joy draining away.

"Theoretically. But only if we had the bad guy's ID card. Otherwise, the UI command won't show up."

"Well, then," she announced in razor-sharp tones, "it's noon. We've got seven hours until the polls close. You, Michael Solano, are going to vote, and *we* are going to track down that card."

The two coders executed sloppy salutes.

"Yes, ma'am," they said.

44

BY 1:00 PM Solano had showered and changed. The trio rolled down the hill into town with Gaffney riding shotgun in Solano's Range Rover. Cassidy followed along in her little Honda.

There were just three voting machines in operation at Solano's polling place, Reno Fire Station #13 in Ward 2, where the polling manager was bemoaning a long and restless line that was moving very slowly.

Solano's heart sank when he saw people strung out along the sidewalk. But even as he took his place at the line's end, it started to shorten up. Disgruntled would-be voters were throwing up their hands and leaving in waves. In just a few minutes he was standing at the intake table with his status verified. The roster specialist, a white haired old man, gave him a voter card. He pushed the card into one of the working machines and dutifully exercised his constitutional franchise.

While he cast his ballot, Cassidy and Gaffney quizzed the assistant manager.

"We've been told that a technician will be here soon. But that was hours ago," wailed the frazzled middle-aged woman.

"We hear about failures all over the city," said Gaffney. "True?"

The woman nodded miserably. "What a mess."

After recording his ballot, Solano glanced at one of the failed machines. As he expected, the touchscreen display read:

```
MACHINE MALFUNCTION CALL TECH SUPPORT
```

Soon after 2:00 PM the anti-fraud squad had visited three more polling places in Ward 2: the visitors lounge at the Home for Mindful Living, the map room of the Tamarack Ranch Interpretive Center, and the main entrance to the Washoe Basin Mall. All three were suffering from multiple voting machine glitches. All three had calls in to the Registrar of Voters, and all three were awaiting onsite technical support.

They moved on to Ward 1, a more conservative area of the city. At the polling station in the High Desert Athletic Club nineteen of twenty machines were up and running. Voters were streaming through.

"Damn," said Solano.

"We are screwed," added Gaffney.

"Next!" said Cassidy.

▼

By now it was 3:00 PM on Solano's Fitbit bracelet. After some debate about heavy traffic, they decided to risk a foray into the far northern reaches of Ward 4.

In the halls of the North Valley Community Center voting was routine. All ten machines were running perfectly, the lines were short, the citizens and polling place workers were proud and happy.

The manager wasn't aware that anyone in the city was having trouble with Patriotic's products.

"Really," said Gaffney, scowling suspiciously. "Machines are screwing up everywhere."

The manager shrugged. "Lucky us."

▼

4:00 PM brought the volunteer investigators through the afternoon's commuter hell to the Gilbert Wheaton School in Ward 3. Seven of the ten machines there were down. Osman Daiyari, the manager, was beside himself. The voters that queued up in the morning were gone. The place was empty. But Patricia Galbraith, his assistant, wasn't giving up, and she had some good news. An ROV technician had just called. He was on his way. Five minutes.

The trio exchanged conspiratorial glances.

Cassidy cleared her throat. "Hate to bother you, but I'm a cop with the Nevada Gaming Control Board."

"Oh yes?"

"Yes, and, um, because of the serious nature of the problems everyone's having, the Registrar of Voters has reached out to several law enforcement agencies for assistance."

Solano and Gaffney backed away from the improvised lie. Cassidy showed Galbraith her ID.

"Oh my Lord. How can I help you, officer?"

Cassidy looked to her companions and wiggled her eyebrows to prompt some assistance. Solano stepped forward.

"When that technician arrives, watch what the screens say when he inserts his ID card," he advised.

"What the screens say . . ." Ms. Galbraith was confused. "Who are you, young man?"

"I'm a technical consultant, working with the officer here."

"Ahh."

"If the screen shows a command like *print demonstration ballot* or *clear paper jam* you don't have to say anything, just give us a big thumbs-up."

"Demonstration ballot? Paper jam? I never heard of them before."

"No, you haven't. They are part of a plot to rig the election."

"A what?"

"A criminal plot, ma'am," emphasized Cassidy.

"God in heaven." She waved to Daiyari. "Oz, Oz — come talk to me."

Daiyari glided over. "What's the problem, Patty?"

"Someone's trying to ruin our election, and we worked so hard!"

Daiyari stared at his visitors. "Election observers are welcome, but they must take their places in the Observer Area." He gestured toward a set of chairs beyond the voting machines.

"Unh-huh, right, here we go," said Cassidy.

"Thumbs up if you see anything," reminded Solano.

Gaffney sprawled across a chair. "There's got to be dozens of techs. What makes you think ours will be the bad guy, huh?"

"The day is getting old. Time to cover tracks?" speculated Cassidy. She reached down and unwrapped a diminutive Walther PK380 pistol from a holster strapped to her ankle. She dropped the clip to check the loads, slammed it home, and worked the slide to chamber a round.

The sight jolted her companions.

"Whoa!" gasped Solano.

"Woman packing heat," whistled Gaffney with a nod of approval.

"Just in case," said Cassidy, jamming the piece into a jacket pocket.

▼

Solano checked his Fitbit: 4:17 PM. "I thought our man was going to be here in five minutes," he grumbled.

Gaffney yawned. "The tech guy's call? Maybe it was just a trick to keep the troops happy."

But no, right at 4:30 on the school's clock, in walked a large man wearing an ROV ID. He was carrying a little box of tools, and he was whistling a little tune. He looked around, spotted Galbraith, and presented himself.

"Tom Flynn, ma'am. How are you today?" he asked breezily.

"Not good," said Galbraith, studying the man's ID card. "Are you going to fix our machines?"

He held up his toolbox. "Going to try."

"You better. We've been down for hours."

Flynn sidled over to the first out-of-order Ridge E-29 unit.

"Well, well, what have we here? Tired machinery, I guess."

Galbraith hesitated to follow, evidently spooked by the idea of passing judgment on another human being. Solano shooed her after the man by frantically waving his arms.

Flynn's ID card was hanging from a lanyard around his neck. He shoved it into the voter card slot. The machine's screen lit up.

"Let's see. Looks like, well hell, it's just a little old paper jam."

Galbraith's thumb jerked upward.

Cassidy sprang forward with her pistol in her hand. She pointed it at Flynn's head.

"Sir. Stop what you are doing and step away."

Flynn's face turned white. He started to put his hands up. But then he yanked his ID card out of the machine and attempted to break it in half. Gaffney came up behind him, grabbed his arms and pulled them backward.

Cassidy fumbled in her pocket and produced a pair of heavy-duty flex cuffs.

Solano zipped the plastic ties around Flynn's wrists.

"There, fucker. Got you now," barked Gaffney.

"Don't know what you're talking about," protested Flynn. He was shaking all over.

"Steady there, buddy," said Cassidy, pushing him into the Observer Area.

The polling place workers were horrified by the violent skirmish and were cringing behind the intake table, all of them pale as ghosts.

Solano waved Flynn's ID card at them. "Hey, you guys, watch me. You gotta see this."

He re-inserted the card in the first malfunctioning unit. As predicted, the mysterious command to *Clear VVPAT Paper Jam* appeared. He pressed a finger on it.

Daiyari and Galbraith slowly approached. After a few seconds, the machine rebooted and declared itself ready for action. They oohed and ahhed.

Solano moved on to the next machine, and then the next.

Anne Weiss, the roster specialist, joined the group. "It's a miracle," she said.

"Now good citizens can make their votes count," said Daiyari.

Solano looked around. All the machines were now operational, but no citizens were waiting to make any votes count.

▼

Cassidy drove Flynn downtown and marched him into police headquarters. The desk sergeant, a middle-aged officer, looked up from a solitaire game on his computer. He made note of Cassidy's weapon, still aimed at her prisoner.

"Hello. What's this?"

Flynn was struggling to get out of his handcuffs. He also had his eyes on Cassidy's little Walther. "I'm innocent. This crazy woman is *crazy*. She's nuts! Insane! Let me go!"

Cassidy kept her gun trained on Flynn while she showed her badge to the cop.

"Gaming Control?" sniffed the desk sergeant. "What did he do? Steal a pile of chips?"

"This man — this loser — was paid to screw up voting machines. He's responsible for knocking out dozens all over Reno, depriving citizens of their lawful right to vote."

"How do you know that?"

"We caught him in the act, over in Ward 3."

The desk sergeant was dubious. "I don't know. Gaming Control? What's your authority to make an arrest?"

Flynn was bouncing up and down. "She doesn't have any. She's out of her mind!"

"Is that right, sister? Are you out of your mind?"

Cassidy's face darkened. "Listen, you. I have no actual authority. But this man is going to be indicted for fraud, plus a bookful of lesser charges, along with a lot of other people, and it will be big news. Don't you want to line up with the good guys on TV?"

The desk sergeant considered the idea. "I can't hold him without some kind of authority. Hell, lady, I'm not telling you anything you don't already know."

"How about this — it's election day, right?"

"Yeah . . ?"

"You voted?"

"On my way in this afternoon. What a zoo, half the stupid machines were down."

"See? That's what I'm trying to tell you — sabotage!"

The desk sergeant sat back in his chair. "If you say so . . ."

"You're a voter, a decent citizen. Be a hero. Stick this guy in the tank until the polls close. After that he can walk."

"Am I deaf? I thought you wanted an indictment."

"We've got his ID, we know where he lives, we'll pick him up when the grand jury votes. How's that?"

The desk sergeant sighed heavily. He put on an ironic grin, smacked his palms on his thighs, stood up reluctantly, and sidled around his desk. "Wait till the chief hears about this."

He grabbed Flynn's arm and led him away.

"All right, my friend, let's take a time out from our busy day."

Cassidy watched the pair march down a long corridor, with the outraged Flynn signifying loudly all the way. "You can't hold me. This is crazy. I work for the county! I've got a job to do!"

The desk sergeant was sympathetic. "There's Coke in the fridge. Cable TV. You can order pizza."

▼

At 5:00 PM, Solano and Gaffney motored by the station and picked up Cassidy. Together they set out to make the rounds of as many polling places as possible. While they negotiated the city streets, Cassidy made calls to the Registrar of Voters office, briefing officials on the situation. They were polite, but incredulous.

"What's the story?"

Cassidy was grim. "They are — quote — going to look into it."

"Bureaucrats! Idiots, they have no idea," griped Gaffney.

"But we've got Flynn's ID card," said Solano. He checked his Fitbit. "And two hours. We better use both. Give me the next stop."

Gaffney consulted his list of vulnerable precincts and directed Solano to the Wild Horse Fitness and Training Facility over near the airport.

Dashing back and forth across the city in the middle of a weekday rush hour, the anti-fraud squad managed to reactivate seventy-three voting machines at sixteen polling places in ninety-odd minutes.

Their final rescue took place in the Downtown Reno Library on

Center Street. They were exhausted by their frantic efforts. Solano shuffled outside and sat himself down on a concrete planter box holding a leafless acacia tree. Cassidy and Gaffney joined him there.

"We did it," said Cassidy, slumping forward with elbows on her knees and face in her hands. "Congratulations to us."

"People leaving work," observed Gaffney, indicating an uptick in pedestrian traffic on the sidewalks. "Now we'll see some action."

They waited. Over the course of fifteen long minutes, only three people showed up to vote.

"I don't see a line anywhere, do you?"

"They probably voted already."

"Or they just don't care."

Cassidy got up and stretched. "So Paxton wins, so what? He's just another cog in the government wheel. Screw him."

"Oh no. No, no, no." objected Gaffney "It's not over. We've still got almost half an hour."

Solano forced a weary smile. "Look, we're downtown, far from home. Everyone's commuting, so hey, they'll vote in the burbs. That's where the lines are."

Cassidy cast a pitying glance in his direction. "You wish. You hope."

Solano hung his head. "Yeah, I do."

45

THE MOROSE VIGILANTES gathered around the five TV monitors in Solano's home office to watch the returns come in. At first, with his Las Vegas totals, Ives shot ahead, and guarded optimism prevailed. They ordered Chinese takeout.

By nine o'clock, results from Reno pushed Paxton into a hair-thin lead. Their food went uneaten.

"It will only get worse when the rural counties weigh in," grumbled Solano. He stomped into the kitchen and removed Cassidy's bottle of champagne from the refrigerator.

"We can't celebrate, but we need to get drunk. Who's ready?"

Cassidy and Gaffney both shook their heads.

"Alcohol is a depressant," said Gaffney. "I'm depressed enough already."

Solano left the champagne bottle unopened on the kitchen counter.

By nine-thirty, all the TV stations were calling the election for Conway Paxton. KNVR ran on-air interviews with both men.

"I refuse to concede until all the paper ballots have been tallied," insisted Ives bravely. A ragged crowd of die-hard supporters behind him cheered.

Paxton was conciliatory. "Senator Ives is a good man who has served Nevada well. But his time is past. There's a new world of opportunity out there, and I'm going to help Nevada seize it." He swept his right arm around in a big victory wave that caused an impressive gathering of his enthusiastic supporters to clap and shout.

A disc jockey hired by the Paxton campaign revved up the Fleetwood Mac song, *Don't Stop*. Everyone started dancing and singing and swatting at the hundreds of red, white, and blue balloons that floated down from the ceiling.

In the KNVR studios, Diego Ramirez stepped in front of the happy scene to summarize the details.

"This was a close race, neck and neck all the way. Paxton has defeated our longtime senator, but his victory is so narrow, he won't have a mandate to carry out his agenda, right, Mags?"

Morrison joined him on camera. "That's the thinking, Diego."

"I've heard some Ives supporters calling for a recount. Is that likely?"

Morrison shook her head. "Probably not. Close as it was, the result is pretty clear. Paxton's margin looks solid."

Ramirez raised a questioning hand. "What are the pundits saying?"

"Well, Diego, it all came down to turnout. It was low this year, as expected. An ugly campaign always suppresses the vote. Who dodged all the mud the candidates were slinging and showed up anyway? Paxton supporters did, and Ives supporters did not."

Solano balled up a sheet of paper and threw it at the screen.

Gaffney angrily prowled around the room, arms flailing. "We've got to hand over our stuff. Get it into the hands of the law. Once the truth comes out, goodbye Paxton."

Solano thought about the situation. "We aren't even sure fraud made the difference. Who gets our evidence? The Reno police? Registrar of Voters?"

Cassidy waved her arms in a time-out gesture. "We've got to be careful. We don't want our actions, possibly illegal, to color the facts."

"What actions? How illegal?" Gaffney was outraged.

Cassidy ticked off some of the possibilities on her fingers. "How about interfering with voting procedures? Or false arrest of a government employee? Or, God help us, illegal possession of proprietary computer software?"

Gaffney collapsed into a chair. Solano grabbed his phone and made a call.

"Cam? You there? Pick up! Don't leave me haunting your voicemail."

After three tries, Solano's lawyer called back. "Mickey? Hard to talk, I'm drunk."

"Hey, Cam, wish I were. Listen, I've got solid evidence of the voting fraud we talked about. Sabotage code written by Frank Osgood, the guy who got himself murdered, all deciphered plain as day, plus his secret passwords, plus the phony ID card used by a voter tech named Tom Flynn to knock out the machines. It's all tied up in a bow."

"Yeah?"

"I'm worried about handing everything to the Registrar of Voters, makes them look bad. They'll bury it."

"Maybe."

"What should we do with this stuff?"

"How many machines did the guy actually tattoo?"

"Hang on . . ." Solano turned to his little team. "How many units did we reboot?"

"Seventy-three," said Gaffney.

Solano nodded. "Cam? Still there? Don't know the total, but we found and fixed seventy-three of those things."

"Jesus Christ on a fucking tortilla. Tell you what, bring everything down to my office — I'm here with Madge, we're celebrating, sort of. Holding a wake."

"What then?"

"I'll make arrangements to hand everything to the Nevada attorney general. That's your best bet."

Solano was hesitant. "Can we trust you?"

"Of course you can."

"For sure?"

"What's the worry?" Hayes was wounded by Solano's misgivings. "Just because I get around, doesn't mean I lie down with dogs. No fleas on me, kiddo. Damn."

"Okay then, on our way."

Gaffney was listening to Solano's end of the call. He nodded approval. "Go, Mick," he said. "Smart move. This is not over, but I'm tired. I'm going home." Without further ado he waved goodnight and stalked out of the house.

Cassidy and Solano made digital copies of all the Patriotic code files. While they were also printing everything out on paper they heard Gaffney's motorcycle rev up and zoom away at an angry speed.

"Your friend has issues," observed Cassidy.

"You could say that," agreed Solano.

▼

Outside, the lights of Reno glittered under a moonless sky. Solano and Cassidy had their incriminating evidence all packaged up in cardboard boxes. They paused to admire the view.

"Beautiful night," murmured Cassidy.

"Yeah." Solano shrugged. "Life goes on."

Their words froze into little clouds in the chilly air.

Solano drove down the hill in a thoughtful mood. He was wondering about the night ahead and how it might involve the woman sitting silently beside him in the passenger seat. He parked his Range Rover beside the Bank of America tower without reaching a conclusion and led Cassidy up to Cameron Hayes' office, cradling the boxed-up fraud evidence like a newborn baby.

After three rings, Madge opened the door. She was wearing a bathrobe. She blushed when she saw Solano and his unannounced companion.

Hayes himself was draped across the office sofa, also in a bathrobe, barely conscious.

"Here, it's okay, I'll take it." Madge lifted the boxes from Solano's arms and stowed them behind her desk.

"Don't let anyone touch that stuff," warned Cassidy.

"Oh no, don't worry. Only Mr. Hayes."

The anti-fraud warriors turned to go. Suddenly Hayes stood up, trying to look alert. When he spoke, his voice was thick and gooey.

"Mickey — there you are, my boy — don't talk to anyone, especially the voting machine company. They'll try to seize their property before we can use it."

"Mum's the word, Cam."

"Same thing with your date here."

"Jaquoya? Don't worry, she's a cop."

"Well, I'll be . . ." The boozy attorney leered at the officer. "She does make law enforcement look attractive. But — *shhh!* — don't let her in on our secret."

Madge rolled her eyes to heaven.

Solano grinned. "So long, you two. Better make that nightcap an espresso."

▼

Solano and Cassidy returned to his Range Rover in silence. The excitement of the day was gone, and their exploits didn't feel like any kind of victory.

"Want to grab a bite somewhere?" he asked robotically.

"Not hungry."

"Me neither," he realized. "Where's your car?"

Cassidy pointed across town.

"Over by the station."

Solano maneuvered his SUV through city streets, under the gaudy Reno Arch, and east to the Reno Police Department. Cassidy's Honda was parked right in front.

"The last time I was here, I almost got shot," he remembered.

"Thanks for the ride," said Cassidy, cracking open her door and sliding out into the night. She sounded tired. Her mind seemed to be drifting to private thoughts. Solano imagined she was holding some sort of internal debate with herself.

"Hey, thank *you* for showing up today," he blurted, at a loss for better words.

"No *problemo.*"

"We should try longboarding again," he continued, mindlessly nattering on. "I know a great slope. Wear your pads."

"Sure, why not?"

She started toward her car, then leaned back into the Range Rover.

"You're a person of interest in a money laundering case, don't forget."

"Uh-oh."

"As such, do not leave town, hear me?"

"Got it."

"I want to know your whereabouts at all times."

He gave her a lopsided grin. "Don't worry, I'll call you."

She tossed her dreads. "Glad we got that straightened out. Now get out of here before I drag your ass to jail."

She slammed the door and walked away. Solano watched her get into her Honda and drive off. For a few minutes afterwards he forgot all about the election.

46

NEWS of the day.

At KNVR-TV, Diego Ramirez and Maggie Morrison were still discussing the senate race, long after it was over.

"What do you make of all the rumors we're hearing, Diego?" prompted Morrison, setting up her co-anchor for the latest political story.

"They grab your attention, if nothing else, Mags."

"Voter fraud? Is it possible?"

The video presentation behind the broadcasters' desk shifted to a computer conference where scruffy young men and women were bent over laptops, working to undermine the nation's voting machines. Suddenly one of them leaped to his feet, hands raised over his head in a triumphant fiero gesture. A closeup of the compromised unit followed. The image on the machine's screen turned into a skull and crossbones. The rest of the group joined in the cheers and jeers.

"Just a couple of weeks ago, at the HackerJack Tournament down in Austin, kids demonstrated the ability to penetrate the security of some of these electronic voting machines in less than an hour."

"Ooh, that's scary."

"There's more . . ."

A police mugshot appeared onscreen. The man in the photo looked old and frightened.

". . . right here in Reno, based on sensational evidence supplied to the Nevada attorney general, a technician identified as one Thomas Flynn of Sparks has been arrested for fraudulently disabling more than a hundred voting machines on election day."

"Why would he do that?" Morrison pretended to be puzzled.

"Suppress turnout."

"In whose favor?"

"Looks like Flynn received money from the Silverlode Casino —

and some of the rumors floating around connect the Silverlode to Paxton's campaign."

Morrison scowled dramatically. "It gets deeper and deeper. Would that be enough to sway the election?"

"Probably not this time. Paxton struck a chord with voters and won by almost twelve thousand votes. At most, the fraud scheme — if true — would have erased nine or ten thousand."

"So democracy still rules? That's my America," said Morrison, looking proud and patriotic.

"Wait'll next year."

Morrison nodded gravely and shifted into her *I'm-serious* public service mode. "Too bad voting machine software isn't subjected to the very strict Nevada standards governing video games."

"You said it, Mags. Patriotic Decision Systems is wearing a big black eye tonight."

After a commercial break announcing that the Mount Rose ski area would open early this year with four lifts running, Morrison continued with more political news.

"Speaking of our new senator-elect, here he is thanking his supporters . . ."

The broadcast cut from the studio to Paxton headquarters and the man himself. His unexpected win had him grinning from ear to ear.

"My friends, I owe you all a huge debt of gratitude for responding so enthusiastically to my message of privatization, my call to turn loose the creative capacity of our citizens, bring us all into the prosperous future we know we deserve.

"I especially want to thank you voters in Reno. You made me a winner — and I'm coming up there to thank you personally this weekend."

The TV camera refocused on Morrison at her studio desk.

"Hear that? Get ready for traffic jams downtown, folks, because Conway Paxton is going to hold a victory rally at the Events Center tomorrow morning.

47

SOLANO WATCHED the news report in a gloomy funk, then poured himself a slug of vodka, drank it fast, and collapsed into bed.

In the morning, a cloudy Sunday, he showered and dragged himself into his office to check the point spread on Monday Night Football. He was depressed, but not hopelessly so, because recent political distractions didn't stop a last-minute bet on the Dodgers from paying off; they won the World Series in five games. True, he was wrong about the election, and his failure grated, but the baseball result suggested that his sixth sense was still working.

One of his TV screens cut away from sports programming to cover Senator-Elect Paxton's imminent arrival at the Reno airport.

A junior reporter for KNVR was there with camera and microphone to marvel at the gathering crowd. He was wearing earmuffs, a scarf, and his breath was coming in visible puffs.

"If you look over my shoulder," he said, "you can see excited Paxton supporters trying to keep warm while they await their hero. Let's hope everyone's wearing their woolies — there's a delay, and our dashing new senator isn't expected for an hour or so. Some problem down in Vegas, I'm told, so back to you, Greg."

In the studio, the morning news anchor traced the planned route of Paxton's motorcade into town on an animated map.

Solano switched channels in disgust. He was busy analyzing the Monday night game, which looked to be close, when his phone rang.

"Guess what, Mick? I'm back in town," came a light voice, professionally honed.

"Gigi!"

"Yup."

"What are you doing here? What about Portland?"

"Just a quick visit this trip. You were right about voter fraud. I'm doing a follow-up for KGW. Hey, I can be seen in public now. We should get together."

Solano's blurry memories of his brief entanglement with the perky reporter snapped back into focus. They sent his mood spiraling downward.

"Um, can't do it, Gigi."

"Why not? What's up?"

"It's awkward . . . . . . I might be seeing someone."

Newhouse slowly absorbed the news. "Seeing someone," she murmured. Then, brightly, "Of course you are!"

"Risky bet, not sure it will pay off . . . sorry . . ."

"Don't be." She paused to collect herself before issuing a crisp farewell. "Right, then — got the message. Take care of yourself, high-rolling dude."

Click.

The line went dead. Solano let out a grumpy sigh. And yet, he noticed a small wound closing, an invisible burden lifting away. He savored the feeling for thirty seconds.

Then his phone rang again. Gaffney calling.

"Bro, can you believe?" See the news? That fuck Paxton rolls to glory and not a word about fraud. It's a fucking — quote — *celebration* — unquote!"

"Take it easy, Bill. Game over."

"Not over! Did you hear the reporter — he actually called that Nazi crook *dashing.* Without the slightest fucking trace of irony."

"Hey, lighten up. I don't think Paxton is actually a Nazi."

"No? Wait till he stages his coup."

"Coup?"

"Could happen. He's got allies. Crazy people with money."

This line of talk made Solano uneasy. The word *crazy* was starting to feel like an accurate description of his raging friend.

"Come on, calm down. He's extreme, granted, but we actually elected the guy." Solano smiled. "He'll be okay — he's *dashing* now."

"We *did not* elect him. That fuck Flynn did the job. He has no right to screw us. And I'm going to do something about it."

"Not a good idea, bud."

"Plan B, Mick. Stay tuned."

Click.

Once again the line went dead. Solano tossed the phone onto his desk and twirled it around with a fingertip. Gaffney, what a nut.

▼

An hour later the gambler was making his first visit to the Silverlode Sports Book since the day Officer Voss got shot.

"I'm taking the points on Monday night, Sparkles," he decided. "The Falcons are good, they're going to win, but it's an away game. They won't cover."

"Attaway, Mick," approved the book manager. "That's more like you. No more suicide bets."

"Nope, those days are over."

Sparling looked around the room for prying eyes and big ears. He leaned close to his good customer.

"You heard about Mr. Barber and Mr. Worden?"

"Of course. That's why those days are over."

Sparling nodded sagely, his idea of recent events starting to jell. "Different kind of management upstairs now, Mick. Muscling players is a thing of the past. Your money? Always good here."

"Thanks, I guess. Maybe someday I'll relax."

"It was all Worden, you know. We weren't as profitable as he would have liked, but Mr. Barber wouldn't hurt a fly."

"Keep the faith, Sparkles. Light a candle if you want. There'll be a trial. I'm taking the points on that too."

▼

On his way out the door Solano glanced at a TV screen swirling with slick advertisements for the Silverlode's gaming tables, restaurants, and bars. Just then it cut to news of Senator-Elect Paxton's private jet landing at the Reno airport. It taxied to the waiting crowd and Paxton stood in the door that opened.

"Good morning, friends!" he shouted to his well-wishers. "I'm here to celebrate a very good morning for Nevada and express my thanks for your solid support!"

He waved, stepped off the plane, and ducked into a long black stretch limousine.

Solano stopped to watch the little ceremony. It reminded him of Gaffney's not-so-veiled threats. He had dismissed them all as idle rants, but now, he remembered — Gaffney owned a gun.

"Oh no," he said aloud. He hefted his smartphone and made a call.

"Morning, Mickey." There was a smile in the answering voice. "Checking in?"

"Jaquoya — where are you?"

"Grand Sierra, at a meeting. HighScore people showing off their latest games, in case you're wondering."

"I'm not. Listen, Bill is on the loose. He won't let go of the election, and he's threatening action."

"Come on, is he serious?"

"How should I know? He's nuts. Mental."

"What we like to say is *reality challenged,* or sometimes, *ninety-six.*"

"Ninety-six, then — with a gun. And Paxton is here in the city, heading for his big rally."

This information sobered Cassidy. "How do you know he has a weapon?" she demanded.

"I saw it on our surveillance trip."

"Okay. Weapon confirmed. Gotta check the crowd," she said. It sounded like an order.

"Big job, are you kidding? Impossible."

"I'll help. Where's the rally?"

"Events Center. The motorcade is coming over from the airport."

"Meet you on Virginia, under the Arch. Five minutes."

48

WILBUR ROLLINS GUYETTE was dozing in his '59 Cadillac. His prized possession was a bulging relic with the tail fins of a rocket ship, and the thing was so long it occupied two parking spaces near the Mini Mart where his janitorial services were recently, and so unfairly, terminated. He was waiting for customers to vacate the premises.

His sleepy thoughts were vengeful. Fired after almost a *year* of faithful employment. So one time he didn't mop the bathroom, so what? And he liberated a candy bar. Not even a bar, just a little tin box of Altoids. Call that a firing offense? Never. The missing case of beer? A setup. Obvious prejudice. If he'd been one of those Mexican beaneaters, well, he'd still be at work. Fuck the owners. Fuck the beaneaters while you're at it. Fuck all.

▼

Conway Paxton was riding westward on Plumb Lane. His limousine was moving slowly, to make sure supporters lining the street recognized him when he stood up through the open sunroof. He was euphoric in victory. His wide and winning smile was genuine. His waving arm was tireless. Except the day was cold, and every now and then he sat down for a few moments to thaw his fingers and ears.

Roger Neff, his campaign manager, and Walter Bascomb, Lloyd Snell's retainer, were riding with him.

"I'll be setting up an office in DC, Roger. You should be in charge."

"That's great. Appreciate your confidence."

"And here's what I'm looking for — old Ivey, he was on the Appropriations Committee. Get me there."

"Should be easy, sir."

"Add Small Business and Entrepreneurship while you're at it."

"Gotta make that campaign rhetoric look good. I'll negotiate."

Paxton turned to Bascomb. "Wally, you did a great job strategizing my run. Don't tell the hoi polloi" — he blew a kiss to a mother of three on the curb — "but I don't plan on a long senate career. Couple of years from now, opportunities could open up."

Bascomb nodded. "That's right, senator. They could. Vice president — as of now, it's a vacuum in the party. You could fill it."

"For starters," said Paxton.

"Starters, right," acknowledged Bascomb.

"I want you to get an office going. It'll take a lot of work."

"Can do, sir."

▼

Bill Gaffney came out of the rundown motel where he was temporarily holed up, sniffed the cold morning air, donned heavy gloves, and aimed his motorcycle toward downtown. He crossed under I-80, cruised down Arlington, dodged left and right through Reno's back streets, and parked on the fifth floor of the Whitney Peak Parking Garage.

There he checked the loads on his pistol. Seventeen 9x19 Safe Action bullets in the clip. He fumbled with the slide and accidentally ejected a cartridge before he managed to coax one into the chamber.

"Okay, baby, we're set," he mumbled.

He wiggled his shoulders and started for the elevator. Under his down jacket he was wearing a bulletproof vest. He had purchased the thing online in case Plan B turned into a firefight. It itched.

▼

Solano legged it from the Silverlode to the Virginia Street Arch, faded and forlorn under gray skies, in no time. There he pushed his way through the gathering throng, across the curb and into the street. He studied the crowd, looking for Gaffney, but either his friend wasn't there, or he was the needle in a human haystack.

He tapped a number on his mobile phone.

"Bill? Talk to me, man."

But Gaffney did not answer.

Moments later a taxi slammed to a halt at the Arch, and Jaquoya

Cassidy leaped out. She nervously scanned the area.

A few yards down the street Solano was still searching for Gaffney. The squelch of taxi tires lifted his gaze, and he spotted the policewoman. She was turning around and around, looking for him. He didn't realize he was holding his breath until he let out a big sigh of relief. He waved. She waved back.

Neither of them stopped to think about it — they rushed together and hugged each other. Then realization dawned, and they sprang apart, faces red with embarrassment.

"Shit, Jaquoya. I tried to call my buddy, but he's not answering. I might not even have his real number."

"Try again. If nothing else, maybe we'll hear a ringtone."

"In this crowd, yelling and screaming?"

"Call him. Who knows?"

Solano made another call. While he listened, Cassidy outlined her own precautions.

"I got the local cops educated. They're on alert, on scene, they've got a description."

Solano eyed the noisy multitude. "Where? I don't see anyone."

"Here. Somewhere. Crap, I don't know."

They were both losing hope of corralling their wild horse.

Solano jammed his phone against his ear. He nodded grimly to the recorded voice and waved the device at Cassidy. "Gaffney on voicemail — his words? — *Justice will be done this day.*"

"God Almighty."

"At least I do have a contact. Maybe he'll call us."

"Maybe. What's your bet, Professor Probability?"

Solano's shoulders slumped. He shook his head. "No call. He's on autopilot, whatever he's up to."

Cassidy snorted. "Honestly, Mickey, the people you hang out with."

"Where's that damn motorcade, anyway?" fretted Solano.

▼

Paxton's limo turned up Virginia Street. The crowd was thinner along the wide thoroughfare, still some distance from the motorcade's destination.

A local policeman on a motorcycle fell back from the lead and rode alongside Paxton's window.

"Got a report on a possible attack, senator."

Paxton cupped an ear. "What? What's that?"

"Possible action, sir. You want to stay buttoned up." The officer had to shout to make himself heard.

Paxton nodded vaguely, gave the cop a thumbs-up. "Thanks. I understand."

But he didn't.

"Hear that, Roger? There's going to be some kind of counter demonstration up ahead."

"Ives is a sore loser. It rubs off on his supporters. It will be rowdy, but we've got more people than he has."

Bascomb chimed in. "Be loud and proud, sir — we won!"

49

ROLLY GUYETTE, still sitting in his Cadillac, had a small water gun in one hand, molded out of orange plastic. He had an oversized felt tip marker in his other hand, which he was using to blacken the gun while he kept watch on the nearby Mini Mart.

When the gun was black and the store's customers had all departed, he got out of his car, marched inside, and threatened the cashier.

"You. Down on the floor."

The cashier was old and timid. To his wide eyes, Guyette's toy looked real.

"Don't shoot!"

He let himself down behind the counter.

"Move over, granddad. Scoot!" commanded Guyette. He gave the old man a kick and opened up the cash register.

"Hey, there's only two hundred bucks in here. Where's the rest of your fucking money?"

The old man pulled his knees up into a fetal position.

"That's all we've got in the till."

"Bullshit."

"Sorry, sorry, no safe in the store. There's a sign on the window."

"Is there now?"

"Oh yes, yes, no more money."

"Well, fuck, I'll just have to take some of your fucking beef jerky then, won't I?"

"Take whatever you want. Have some beer. Take everything!"

Guyette filled his pockets with bills, beef jerky, and little bottles of 5-Hour Energy Drink.

"Now stay put for ten minutes, or I'll come back and shoot you. Hear me, what I'm saying?"

The old man closed his eyes, squeezing out tears.

"No trouble. Not gonna move."

"All right, then. Tell the owners, fuck them."

Guyette headed for the exit. Once he was out of sight around the counter, the old man reached up and pressed a hidden button. Alarm bells clanged. The hammering clatter was deafening.

Guyette was startled. He sprinted for his car. As he took the wheel, he could hear police sirens, not ten blocks away, getting louder. He checked his rear view mirror. Blue and red lights were approaching at high speed.

"My fucking luck," he wailed, and stomped on the accelerator.

The Cadillac's tires chirped, and the monster machine roared away like the rocket it resembled.

▼

Five floors up in the parking garage, the elevator slowly opened its doors for Bill Gaffney. He stepped inside and pressed the *lobby* button, nervously fidgeting with the gun in his belt.

The doors remained open. He jabbed at all the controls, but nothing happened. Finally, the doors closed on their own, and the car started to descend. Somewhere in the shaft, metal was grating against metal. The elevator cables were twanging.

"Don't they ever call maintenance around here?" he grumbled.

The car lurched downward. Past the fourth floor, past the third floor, past the second floor. Then, part way between the second floor and the lobby, it suddenly jolted to a halt. Gaffney almost fell over.

"Whoa!"

He punched the lobby button repeatedly. No joy. Then the lights went out.

"What the hell?"

He dug out his mobile phone, activated the flashlight, and examined the elevator's control panel. Down at the bottom he discovered a yellow button for emergencies sitting between a tiny speaker and a tiny microphone.

He pressed the yellow button, and a metallic voice spoke.

"Kannik hem jooz?"

Man or woman talking? He couldn't tell. Where from? Somewhere remote. Maybe, he thought with a sinking heart, all the way from a call center in faraway India.

"Hello? Hello?"

"Tallum yurge proburk."

"Hello? Hey, I'm trapped in your elevator."

"Wargham?"

"Where am I? That your question?"

He ran the flashlight over the elevator interior.

"Yeah, where?"

The beam picked out a sign on the control panel.

"Uhh, looks like I'm stuck in Car Number Four, Whitney Peak Garage." Thinking about India made him add, "in Reno, Nevada, U-S-A."

"Stakkam. Zend kroo."

"Damn well better. I'm armed. If they're not here in five minutes I'm going to shoot my way out, got that?"

"Burzzz."

He stood waiting in the dark. In the distance he could hear the cheers of a crowd — and then, a little later, the muted howl of distant police sirens.

▼

Rolly Guyette was racing north on Arlington with police vehicles closing in. Code three lights were flashing, and sirens were shrieking. Bullhorns were blaring stern orders to pull over, but Guyette paid no heed. He laid a hand on his horn, scattering startled pedestrians on every block.

He crossed the river doing fifty miles an hour, skidded around onto 2nd Street, narrowly missing a Jeep, which plowed into a parked Toyota Highlander. The Cadillac's cushy springs and Guyette's panic caused him to wobble almost uncontrollably back and forth across both lanes of travel.

▼

Solano and Cassidy were running up Virginia Street, shouting Gaffney's name. The crowd awaiting Paxton's arrival glared balefully at the duo as if they were hecklers from the defeated Ives faction.

▼

In the stalled elevator car, Gaffney leaped to his feet as urgent voices approached. Someone out there banged on the door. He banged back. Then a steel wedge worked its way in between the door and the doorjamb at about knee height. Fingers followed, pulling hard. With much grunting and groaning, the door creaked open. Gaffney looked down on two workmen standing in the lobby. The elevator was only a couple of feet off the ground.

"Watch out, guys! I'm late."

"How's that?"

Ignoring his rescuers, Gaffney jumped out and sprinted for the sidewalk.

▼

Paxton's limousine approached the intersection of Virginia and 2nd Street at not much more than a walking pace. He was standing up again, with his head, shoulders, and arms thrust up through the open sunroof. He waved and smiled. The crowd waved back.

Solano and Cassidy stopped to watch a small fleet of motorcycles lead the senator-elect and his mobile entourage past them.

Gaffney was on the run a block away. By the time he reached Virginia Street, Paxton's parade had already gone by, so he slowed to a walk.

"Well, damn. I can't watch this crap."

He almost turned away. But then he summoned his resolve and picked up the pace. "Still a chance," he decided. "Maybe he'll bless the crowd or something."

He cocked an ear. What's with the sirens?

▼

Guyette's Cadillac was flying along 2nd Street. It arrived at the Virginia Street intersection at the exact moment Paxton's ride was passing by.

The crowd got an eyeblink's glimpse of impending doom and scattered in panic as the speeding Cadillac careened into the senator-elect's limousine, like a torpedo hitting a ship below the waterline.

KA-BLAMMM!

The impact blasted the limousine onto its right side. Paxton was thrown from the open sunroof. He sailed through the air and crashed through the window of a pawn shop. Shards of glass flew every which way.

A cloud of oily steam rose from the twisted metal and torn hoses on the Cadillac. After a few seconds, tongues of flame appeared under the limousine.

Solano and Cassidy raced to the scene. They pushed through the crush of stunned onlookers and saw one of the motorcycle patrolmen struggling to pry open the limo's left rear door, now a bent-up hatch on the car's high side.

"Oh my God!"

Solano surprised himself by instinctively leaping forward to help. He tore off his belt and wrapped it around the rear door handle. Bracing his feet on the underside of the limo, he tugged and tugged. The motorcycle patrolman took a hand. Finally a second officer joined them and, with all three pulling as hard as humanly possible, the door popped open.

One of the officers leaned inside, reaching for the limo's trapped occupants. Solano held his legs while the man got a grip. One by one the threesome lifted Neff, Bascomb, and the driver out of harm's way.

The cops who were chasing Guyette moved their vehicles into position to block off the intersection. They dropped flares and backed the crowd away.

Within minutes emergency responders were swarming. EMTs bounded out of their ambulances and went to work on the figures lying on the asphalt.

It took some time for the rescue pros to figure out Paxton's resting place. They rolled him out of the pawn shop on a gurney. There was a blanket covering him from head to foot.

"Oh crap," moaned Cassidy. "That man is D-R-T."

Rolly Guyette was knocked unconscious by the collision. His limp form was still behind the wheel. A policeman checked on him, noticed blood all over his face, decided he was down for the count, and hurried off with a fire extinguisher to help control the situation.

Now Guyette's eyes fluttered open. He moved his tongue around a mouthful of broken teeth. He blinked at the star-shaped crack in the windshield. He touched a hand to his forehead. It came away bloody.

"Urrghhh," he gurgled.

He shouldered the door open and stood up. Everyone's attention was on Paxton's limo and the drama surrounding it. Time to move. He limped around the tail end of his ruined car and dragged himself toward the sidewalk.

Suddenly a heavy body came flying out of nowhere, hit him hard and sent him sprawling. Guyette's head whacked the pavement, and stars swirled through his vision. When he opened his eyes he was staring up at the barrel of a Glock 17.

The gun was held and aimed by his burly assailant, Bill Gaffney.

"Do not move, asshole," ordered the would-be political assassin.

A uniformed cop came running to referee the standoff. Gaffney was grateful to hand over his captive.

"He's yours, officer," he said, coolly hiding his gun in a jacket pocket. "Driver of the big boat over there."

The cop looked confused. Then he noticed the blood and bruises. He snapped a pair of steel handcuffs around Guyette's limp wrists.

Meanwhile, Solano and Cassidy were riveted to the unfolding crisis. Firemen had arrived and were fighting the blaze under the limo.

They were working to keep it away from the vehicle's recent occupants, who were still scattered about on the ground, each one attended by a knot of paramedics. CPR and defibrillators were in use. The prospects looked grim.

Solano felt a tap on his shoulder. He looked around.

"Hey, bro. Some rally, huh?"

It was Gaffney, looking sheepish.

"Bill — ! Shit, man, where you been?"

"Stealth mode, kind of busy."

Cassidy scowled. "Oh really?"

Gaffney winced. He looked around at all the blue uniforms, reached into his jacket, and hauled out his Glock. He dangled it by the heel of the grip in front of Cassidy.

Solano stared darkly at the thing. "This? This was Plan B?"

"Yeah."

Cassidy delicately took the offered gun, dropped the clip out, cleared the chamber, and stuffed it into her own jacket.

"You moron, you had us going crazy," she said.

"I know. I was going to get involved." He shrugged like a guilty kid.

"But instead, how about I buy you both a beer. I need one."

50

NEWS of the day.

The KNVR news anchors were recounting the day's dominant events with long faces and long stories.

A storm was moving into the Sierra; snow was falling above forty-five hundred feet. A small airplane was down near Washoe Lake. Three people had succumbed to carbon monoxide gas from an unventilated heater in Fallon, and the Oakland Raiders had won another football game. None of these stories, each grist for the video mill on any other night, had a chance to air, because all journalistic attention was focused on the Paxton tragedy.

Diego Ramirez summarized the situation in the studio. "Police have identified the cause of the collision as one Wilbur Rollins Guyette, driving with an expired license, who was being chased from the scene of a robbery. This calls into question, once again, police policy in regard to hot pursuit. What do you think, Maggie?"

The video feed switched to Morrison, who was on location at the intersection of Virginia and 2nd Streets. She was all bundled up in a stylish winter jacket, with a wool hat pulled down over her ears.

"New policy? Stranger things have happened. I'm out here tonight, because even now, hours after the incident, police still have the intersection blocked. That yellow tape is everywhere. Lots of strobes flashing, as you can see, plus these portable construction lights set up to help workers make sense out of a senseless act. And look, here comes a tow truck to haul away Paxton's limousine . . ."

The camera panned around to show the towing crew hook a chain through the B-column of the limo, attach it to their winch, and reel it in. The tow truck engine roared, sheet metal groaned, and the crunched-up stretch toppled back onto its wheels, shedding a cloud of ugly dust as it bounced around.

"I'm told the airbags did deploy, but Paxton's car, rented for the occasion from Royal Transport, wasn't equipped with side bags. Sadly, none of the occupants was wearing a seat belt."

The tow truckers hooked up the limo and slowly hauled it away.

Back in the studio, photos of the victims appeared behind Ramirez, one after another in a repeating cycle. The anchor sorted through the notes on his laptop.

"Here's the situation as we now understand it," he said. "Paxton was killed instantly, as we have been reporting all evening. Roger Neff, who organized his campaign, died on route to the hospital. The limousine driver, Octavio Perez, and Walter Bascomb, a Paxton advisor, are both in critical condition tonight, as is the driver of the colliding automobile. Miraculously, no one in the crowd was injured by the vehicles themselves. Fourteen bystanders were cut by flying glass, but only two required medical treatment. All have been released."

He paused for a respectful five seconds of silence.

"Now let's go back to my co-anchor, get the latest."

Morrison was standing in front of Guyette's old car. "This is what caused the whole thing. You can hardly tell."

Indeed, to an untutored eye the big Cadillac looked repairable, if not immediately drivable. The hood was rippled, the bumper was twisted against the remains of the grill, one tire was flat, and one headlight was shattered. A tow truck hauled it away while she was describing the damage.

Morrison opened her arms to bitterly embrace the entire intersection and all the residual activity. "Tell me, tell our viewers out there, how we are going to recover from Paxton's tragic loss."

Ramirez cleared his throat.

"It's pretty simple. The governor will appoint someone to fill Paxton's seat. Then, next November, we'll hold another election —"

"Hey, Diego, look!" Morrison exclaimed, interrupting. She held out a hand, palm up. "It's snowing!"

So it was. Soft flakes were floating down, shimmering in the glare of the work lights.

Back in the studio, Ramirez attempted a wan smile. "That's great, Mags. Don't catch cold."

▼

In bed in his house on Lake Tahoe, Solano was lying on his back with his hands behind his head. He was propping himself up to watch the grim news. As the accident coverage wound down, and a hastily composed montage of Paxton's rise to fame took over, he thumbed his TV remote to check the weather channel.

"Hey, you — snow tonight, clearing in the morning," he called out. "We will be boarding the white stuff on Mount Rose!"

His master bathroom door opened, and Jaquoya Cassidy emerged. "Can't wait," she said.

She was naked. She paraded across the room with her dreadlocks flopping and her wide hips swaying. Solano watched her approach with an appreciative eye and a big smile.

She lifted the covers and snuggled down underneath. After staring at the ceiling for a moment, she turned toward Solano and pressed her breasts against his chest. He gasped.

"Okay, Mickey — I'm looking at laundered money, a hit that missed, two Silverlode indictments, that voting machine nonsense, our hard work chasing down the fraud, the car crash — wow, that's a lot of shit — what did you learn from it all?"

Solano leaned over and planted a kiss.

"Not much, I guess. Here I am in bed with a cop."

▲ ▲ ▲

www.ingramcontent.com/pod-product-compliance
Lightning Source LLC
Chambersburg PA
CBHW071131200626
46817CB00018B/2670